The storm sprang up out of nowhere. First the wind came, pinching and jabbing at the sails. The waves seemed to sharpen, cutting at the sides of the boat like a thousand metal scythes. Then the clouds rolled in, forming an impenetrable barrier that blotted out the sun and locked the *Success* in a swelling darkness. The thunder tried to break in, pounding against the clouds with invisible fists. Cracks appeared, brilliant silver against the ugly black sky. The ship began to turn – now one way, now another – out of control . . .

The stirring tale of Jack Vincent, one-time officer, one-time gentleman, now turned smuggler, convict and adventurer was written for television by Richard Carpenter, creator of the thrilling *Robin of Sherwood* series. His previous credits include *Dick Turpin*, *Catweazle* and *The Ghosts of Motley Hall*. Anthony Horowitz is a television scriptwriter and has written several thrillers for young adults.

ADVENTURER

ADVENTURER

Anthony Horowitz

From the television script by
Richard Carpenter

CORGI BOOKS

ADVENTURER

A CORGI BOOK 0 552 524492

First publication in Great Britain

PRINTING HISTORY
Corgi edition published 1987

This book is set in 11/12 pt Century
by Colset Private Limited, Singapore.

Corgi Books are published by Transworld Publishers
Ltd., 61–63 Uxbridge Road, Ealing, London W5 5SA,
in Australia by Transworld Publishers (Australia) Pty.
Ltd., 15–23 Helles Avenue, Moorebank, NSW 2170,
and in New Zealand by Transworld Publishers (N.Z.)
Ltd., Cnr. Moselle and Waipareira Avenues,
Henderson, Auckland.

Made and printed in Great Britain by
Cox & Wyman Ltd., Reading, Berks.

1

Knifing through the waves, the little fishing boat cut a straight line for the shore. As if to light it on its way, the clouds rolled back and a bright moon shone down. Most travellers would have welcomed it, for the coast was lined with sharp, jagged rocks — but the man who stood at the helm of the boat clutching the rudder looked up and frowned. He knew his way and needed no help. And the sort of work he was currently engaged in would have been better served by darkness.

There were two men waiting for him on a grey ribbon of a beach. One of them saw the boat clearly silhouetted against the moon. He turned round and pulled a lantern out of a cart. It burned with a dull yellow flame. Twice he swung it in the air, then hid it away in case it was seen by the wrong pair of eyes.

The man in the boat saw it and turned his boat towards it. As a wave lapped underneath the stern, there was a soft, solid thud — wood striking wood. A barrel had slipped. There were more than a dozen of them, small wooden barrels piled high against the sides.

It was a cold autumn night. The new century, the nineteenth century, had barely had time to warm up. The cliffs that soared above the fishing

7

boat and its barrels were the cliffs of Cornwall. The three men were smugglers.

Now one of them moved forward and waded into the water, waiting for the boat to draw near. He was the tub-man, so called because it was his job to unload the tubs or barrels. He was a small, stocky man with swollen muscles and a leering smile.

'Fine night, Jack,' he muttered as the boat drew abreast.

The first man nodded and scanned the beach with cold, watchful eyes. He was younger than the tub-man and yet, in a strange way, his superior. He seemed almost out of place in this midnight operation. The strong, handsome face beneath the dark, curling hair would have been better suited to a London club or coffee house. A nobleman? He certainly wasn't a fisherman like the others.

There was nobody in sight, not a sound apart from the waves dashing themselves mercilessly against the rocks. Satisfied, the man called Jack slid himself over the edge of the boat and into the shallow water.

Together, the three unloaded their cargo, stacking the barrels in the cart for the next stage of the journey. They worked without speaking. Once they had reached the safety of an inn and a roaring fire with perhaps one of those same barrels broached and the contents warming their stomachs, then they might talk and laugh. For the moment they just wanted to be finished and away.

About half the barrels were loaded before the trap was sprung.

It was as if the shadows lying flat in the sand

suddenly sprang up with a life of their own. They came out of nowhere, forming themselves out of the darkness, but suddenly the beach was full of them, men in uniforms carrying heavy sticks, running from all sides towards the cart. Somewhere, someone blew a whistle. Then more men appeared on horseback, the hooves thundering silently into the sand.

'Sharks!' The cart driver spat the word out savagely.

'Curse 'em!' whispered the tub-man.

The three smugglers scattered and ran, Jack drawing a cutlass as he searched desperately for some way out of the rapidly closing net. But the customs officers had planned their night's work too well. Jack had covered only a hundred yards before the first of the riders was on him. He thrust out with his cutlass. There was a cry and the man fell. But then two more loomed up in front of him. There were three others on each side. As Jack stood panting, his blade glinting in the moonlight, they surrounded him, their own weapons raised. Jack twisted round, daring them on.

Then the circle closed.

'The running of contraband along these coasts causes serious losses to this country's revenue — revenue essential to finance our defences against those revolutionary forces who seek destruction of all that is held sacred by loyal Englishmen.'

The judge was old. His face seemed to hang in creases and his skin was the colour of the wood that surrounded him. But his voice rang out across the crowded courtroom and his eyes shone with indignation. A bruised and somewhat

9

ragged smuggler faced him from the stand. But if Jack felt any emotion, he didn't show it. He knew what was coming. He had been playing for high stakes and he had just lost.

'Those, whose personal greed brings in such dutiable goods unlawfully, are little better than traitors.' The judge paused, allowing the silence to hang in the air. 'Jack Vincent,' he went on, 'I sentence you to transportation for the rest of your natural life.'

Jack Vincent was the son of an admiral. Had his father been able to see his son now, he would have spun in his grave — although that grave was of the watery sort, for the old man had died in action at sea. Jack had been a lieutenant himself ... until the day he had taken on a French frigate in his own small brig, the *Cassandra*. It had been an act of heroism. He had actually destroyed the larger ship. But it had also been an act of defiance. He had disobeyed orders and killed half his crew. Jack wasn't honoured on his return to England. He was tried in a court of inquiry and forced to resign his commission.

After that he moved to the village of Keyhaven in the West Country. It was the start of a self-imposed exile that had only ended when he had become friendly with the local fishermen. They were poor, and the new tax on salt had made them poorer still as salt was essential to their livelihood of curing fish. From sympathizer to smuggler had been a small step for Jack. He wanted to help. He had no reason to love the authorities. And at heart he was an adventurer.

And now Jack Vincent had returned to sea — not as an admiral or a lieutenant but as a common prisoner, number forty-one, manacled and locked into a cage hardly big enough for a dog. Even so he was forced to share it with three others, dressed in grey and manacled like himself. Cells lined the narrow passage deep in the bowels of the ship, each one so full as to be crowded. A grim smile tugged at Jack's lips. There would be more room by the time they reached New South Wales; a number of the convicts would not survive the journey.

Meanwhile, two men were watching him. One was old, a grizzled ox of a man in his forties with a balding head and bad teeth. At some time in the past his nose had been broken and had set crookedly. His arms were covered in burns. For a long while he stared at Jack, his eyes suspicious, searching. Then, as if dismissing the thought, he turned away and curled up to sleep.

The other man was in the same cell as Jack. He was actually hardly more than a boy, in his early twenties, thin and edgy with fair, curling hair. Every movement he made, the way his eyes darted from side to side, showed that he was terrified by what lay ahead. To hide his fear he talked. It seemed that he would never stop talking.

'Allow me to introduce myself,' he said to Jack. 'Patrick Cassidy. Pat. Late of the prison hulks at Woolwich.'

Jack propped himself up on one elbow. 'What's your offence?' he asked.

'Being Irish,' Pat replied. 'I'm a Limerick man — like these two.' He gestured at the other two convicts in the cell. 'We're Limerick men. So one night we're taking a little walk in the moonlight but unfortunately it's after curfew. I leave

11

the rest to your imagination, sir. Have you ever been to Ireland?'

Jack shook his head.

'Oh, it's a grand place,' Pat went on. 'Grand. Over-populated and underfed. And the national sport is killing each other. Though we've the English to thank for that. So what brings you on this little trip, if you don't mind me asking?'

'I was a smuggler.'

'Say "freetrader" — it sounds much more dignified. Like "patriot" sounds better than "rioter" or "rebel". It's wonderful what words can do for a man . . .'

But Jack wasn't listening any more. He was suddenly aware that something had changed. Cursing the fact that there was no window for him to see out of, he rested his hands on the floor of the cell. Now he knew what it was. The ship was swaying. Not the short, choppy swaying that he had grown used to in the port but a smoother, rolling movement. It could only mean one thing.

'We're under way,' he said.

The Irishman stopped in mid-sentence, his eyes widening. 'May God have mercy on us!' he whispered and finally fell silent.

For the first few weeks, God did indeed have mercy on them. The wind blew behind HMS *Success* and the convict-ship darted across a smooth sea on its journey south. It was a three-masted brigantine, a naval ship rather than a merchantman that had been specially converted to carry its unwilling cargo.

As soon as they were out of the port, the boatswain — a short, stocky man by the name of

12

Flack — unlocked the convicts' manacles. With the English coast a mere speck on the horizon, they had nowhere to run. And unless they were mad enough to try and swim for it, it was something they would never see again.

The convicts were treated roughly but not brutally, unless they were slow on their feet or spoke out of turn. Then they would get a taste of the boatswain's 'starter', a short length of rope that could lash out like a whip. Much of the time they were left locked in their cells. But even the cruellest guard dared not leave them there too long. The diseases that could start with them might well reach the officers' quarters, and then they would all be lost.

So the convicts were taken out and exercised, forced to run on the spot in the narrow confines of the deck. The ship's surgeon checked them over, opening their mouths and prodding at their teeth as if they were animals rather than humans. Once a week they were washed — a cold shower with the water hurled at them from wooden buckets while they stood, fully dressed and shivering.

And all the time they were watched by a cold, emotionless figure who stood on the quarter deck above them, his eyes seemingly far away. You could tell at once that he was the commanding officer on board — and not just by his perfectly creased, perfectly clean blue and white lieutenant's uniform with its double row of perfectly polished gold buttons. Everything about the man screamed his authority. The way he stood. The way he spoke. The way he smiled.

He didn't smile often, but he was smiling now. It was not a pleasant smile nor even a very humorous one. Down below, the prisoners were exercising. The starter was lashing out to encourage them. Jack Vincent was among them.

The lieutenant had recognized him.

The convicts were playing pontoon, using homemade cards whose faces were barely visible in the glow of the single lamp. They were quieter than they had been when they set out, as if they had left some vital part of themselves back home in England. Nobody said anything as a ladder was lowered into the corridor and the short, knotted legs of Mr Flack appeared, climbing down.

'Forty-one!' he announced.

Jack looked up. And in the cell opposite, the grizzled man who still took a personal interest in the smuggler watched and listened.

'Out!' the boatswain demanded, unlocking the cell.

'What's this about?' Jack asked.

'Out!' Mr Flack didn't like questions — not when they came from convicts.

Jack followed the boatswain up on to the main deck, past the mizzen mast to a low wooden door. Mr Flack knocked.

'Come!'

Lieutenant Anderson was eating a piece of fresh pork with two vegetables, and drinking a bottle of wine. It was a world apart from the dried fish and ship's biscuits that Jack and the other convicts had lived on for the past five weeks. But Jack wasn't looking hard at the food. He was looking at Anderson.

'So it wasn't enough to be thrown out of the Service,' Anderson began as soon as the boatswain had gone. 'It wasn't enough to disgrace your family name. You had to disgrace yourself

14

even further.' He sipped his wine and smiled again. 'I always knew you'd come to a bad end.'

'Did you?' Jack asked impassively.

'I never liked you.' Anderson lowered the wine glass, twiddling with the stem between finger and thumb. 'I thought when I married your sister it might forge a bond between us,' he continued. 'But you had to turn her against me . . .'

'No, Harry. You did that.'

'You believed her vicious flights of fancy?' Anderson raised a cynical eyebrow.

'I believed the vicious marks on her neck.' Jack was fighting to keep control of himself. This man had almost destroyed his younger sister. Two years of marriage to him had reduced her to a weeping, terrified shadow of herself.

'I was surprised to find you were part of my cargo,' Anderson said.

'And I was just as surprised to find you in command,' Jack admitted. 'I was looking forward to New South Wales, but knowing your skills as a navigator, we'll probably finish up in China.'

Anderson laughed at the insult. 'We're not heading for New South Wales, Jack,' he said. 'We're going to the penal colony on Norfolk Island.' Suddenly the laughter was gone and he was staring malevolently across the table. 'You know, what looked like being a tedious voyage has suddenly become . . . full of promise.'

'Put me back in the cells and forget I'm on board,' Jack said. There was a note of warning in his voice. 'Forget we were brother officers. Forget you ever knew me. Because if you don't, if you turn this into some kind of revenge . . .'

He got no further. Anderson's voice cut in like a whip. 'You're hardly in a position to threaten

15

me,' he hissed. 'I always believed your arrogance covered a miserable lack of character and now I have the opportunity to prove it,'

'You haven't changed.' Jack eyed his old enemy wearily. 'You're as big a blaggard as you ever were.'

'I've six or seven months to prove my point.' The smile was back on Anderson's face. 'Mr Flack!' he called out.

The boatswain had been waiting outside the door. Now he stepped back into the room.

'Confine this scum to the cable tier for a month!' Anderson commanded.

Jack felt his stomach flutter and the strength drain out of his legs. He was shocked . . . afraid. But his face gave nothing away. The boatswain, however, was scratching his head and staring at his captain as if the man had just gone mad. The cable tier — the tiny room where the anchor cables were stored — was below the level of the sea. It was cold and grimy with salt water slopping about, six inches deep on the floor. It was pitch dark. And if there was one place on the ship to find rats, the cable tier was where you'd start. A month! A man would be lucky to survive in there for a week.

'Are you sure, sir?' he asked.

'Of course I'm sure, boatswain. Just do it!'

The boatswain sighed and clamped his hand on Jack's shoulder. Jack didn't resist as he was led out of the cabin. But his eyes were fixed on Anderson. If revenge was what Anderson had in mind, then Jack Vincent would survive to the bitter end to seek his own.

* * *

Another four weeks passed. The ship made good progress and it looked as if, despite Jack's taunts, Anderson would lead them to their destination ahead of schedule. It was four weeks in which Pat, the Irishman, babbled to anyone who would listen and another convict called Mason started working on a picklock.

The captain might have forgotten about Convict Forty-one altogether. Perhaps that had been his plan. But it was the boatswain who reminded him. Mr Flack had often wondered about the man called Jack Vincent, and what link there might be between him and the captain. He had thought of him, lingering in the dark, filthy hole, and more than once he had come upon his men taking bets. What would kill Convict Forty-one first — the cold, the solitude or the rats?

'Ah yes,' Anderson said, when Mr Flack told him the month had passed. 'He's still alive?'

'He was at eight bells, sir, when we slung in his grub.'

'Then let's have a look at him shall we, Mr Flack?' Anderson got lazily to his feet, determined that Jack should suffer every last second of his sentence.

A few minutes later, Jack was pulled up on to the main deck more dead than alive. Indeed, many of the crew crossed themselves in the sure belief that they had just dragged a corpse to the surface, as if from his grave. Anderson, however, was less moved. With a well-polished shoe he prodded at the pale, filthy figure, rolling him over so that he faced the sun.

'Oh your feet, Forty-one!' he snarled.

Jack didn't move. He couldn't move.

'If you don't get up, I'll have the skin taken off your back!'

Slowly, painfully, Jack got to his knees. His clothes were in rags, his flesh raw and bleeding where the rats had bitten at him in the dark. But mustering every ounce of his strength he managed to stand, swaying on his feet and blinking in the light.

Anderson smiled maliciously. 'I trust you've learnt your lesson, Forty-one,' he said.

There was a long silence. Jack's lips moved but no sound came out.

'Louder.'

'Yes, sir.'

The two words were a whisper, but they were enough. Anderson nodded, his eyes still fixed on his enemy. 'Take him below!' he commanded, then spun on his heels and walked away.

At once two of the boatswain's mates stepped forward and half-carried, half-dragged Jack back under the deck and into his cell. The other convicts stared at him in silence as slowly, every movement an effort, he turned over and hunched up his legs. It was a silence broken, as always, by Pat.

'Sure and we thought you'd never live through it,' he said.

Jack's eyes flickered open. 'It's not over,' he whispered.

'Holy Mary!' Pat shook his head. 'What more can he do to you?'

'He'll think of something,' Jack muttered painfully.

But the next torment came not from the captain but from an even more unpredictable source. The weather changed. First came two days of storms.

18

For thirty-six hours the boat pitched about in a frenzy with the waves whipping it on and the wind howling at it. The sailors cursed and heaved at the sails. The convicts prayed. Then the wind dropped and the sun broke through the clouds. But if the voyagers on the *Success* were grateful, it wasn't for long. The wind disappeared altogether and the sails hung limp. They were becalmed in an ocean that was suddenly a vast mirror reflecting the heat of the sun until it burned through to the bone.

Anderson ordered water rationing — the convicts getting half as much as the crew who got half as much as him. But even so the water-barrels ran low. It was a crushing sort of heat. Sweating and scratching, the crew moved about like old men.

Then came something even worse. The flux — a sort of dysentery that could spread like the plague and kill just as quickly. It started with the convicts and brought Towers, the ship's surgeon, scuttling in panic to Anderson's cabin.

'Three of the convicts have it,' he reported. 'They're dying, sir.'

'Dysentery's like a forest fire,' Anderson remarked. 'I've seen what it can do on other ships, Mr Towers. I want them overboard.'

The surgeon was too astonished to speak. His mouth flapped open. He was an elderly man with grey hair and a lined, weather-beaten face. He had worked as a ship's surgeon for thirty years. In all that time he had never heard anything like this. 'They're still alive!' he said at last.

'Do you want me to lose the whole damned lot?' Anderson snapped. 'If you can't cure an animal, you put it down.'

'But they're not animals ...' Towers protested.

'They are my responsibility. Mine, Mr Towers! And I say they go overboard. Send for the bo'sun.'

Three men died that night, thrown over the side of the ship into the darkness. Death also came for Jack Vincent. But it wasn't the death of disease.

Jack was asleep, a troubled, suffocating sleep beneath the hot blanket that the air had become. The other convicts lay sweating and groaning in the stench of their cells. But one man was wide awake. It was Mason, the man who had been watching Jack from the start. Now he remembered where he had seen him before. Jack Vincent! It was a name he wasn't likely to forget. It was a man with whom he had long wanted to get even.

Mason had made himself a picklock from a nail he'd managed to loosen from his bunk. Using the same skills that had got him transported in the first place, he pressed it into the lock of his cell and gave it a sharp twist. The lock snapped open.

On tiptoe he crept across the gloomy passage, arriving a moment later at Jack's cell. Once again he twisted the nail. The second door swung open. He stepped inside, the picklock gripped in his hand. Slowly, he raised it . . .

Mason reeled back as Jack's foot lashed out into his stomach. The snapping of the first lock had awoken him. His eyes had been open all the time. The picklock was sent hurtling into the shadows, but Mason was a strong man. Springing forward he managed to get his hands round Jack's throat. Jack pitched himself forward. The two men burst out of the cell into the corridor and sprawled on the floor.

'Don't be a damned fool, Mason!' Jack hissed.

The other convicts were awake now, clustered round their cell doors, enjoying the spectacle. After eleven weeks on the ship they would have welcomed anything to break the monotony.

'Know who we've got here?' Mason called out, addressing them all. 'A real silk stocking gentleman.' He spat at Jack. 'You poxy-eyed swine,' he went on. 'How many died on the *Cassandra* that morning because you wanted glory? Twenty-eight. Twenty-eight!'

Jack's eyes narrowed. He hadn't recognized Mason before but now he saw there was something familiar about the man's face. And the burnt arms should have told him more. The burns had come from the flashes of the cannons. Of course! Mason had been gun captain on the brig *Cassandra*.

'Know what he did?' Mason shouted at the other convicts. 'Attacked a forty-gun frigate with twice our range. Sailed up to her, bold as brass while she blew half the gun deck to kingdom come.'

'We sank that frigate,' Jack reminded him.

'I sank it!' Mason countered. 'Me and my mates! Took her clean through the magazine. Another couple of minutes and there'd have been none of us left — you glory-seeking murderer!'

Mason got to his feet, then with a roar charged at Jack again. Jack's shoulders crashed against the bulkhead, but at the same time his knee came knifing up between Mason's legs. Mason yelled. All the convicts were shouting now, encouraging one man or the other. It was a racket that could have been heard a mile away and nobody was surprised when the boatswain and four mates came running down the ladder to see what was going on. Even so it took another six of them to separate the fighters, Mr Flack lashing out with his starter, first at Jack, then at Mason, then at any other convict unwise enough to be within reach. But at last the two men were clamped down. Flack stared at them, his chest heaving, the sweat trickling off his chin.

'Lock 'em up!' he ordered. 'In the morning they see the captain.'

'I'm hanging the man who made this,' Anderson said.

He was holding the picklock Mason had lost in the course of the fight, which had been found by the bosun. But neither Jack nor Mason were talking.

'Well? Mason? Vincent?' Anderson waited, then nodded to himself. It was nothing less than he had expected, and in a way he was glad. To have hanged Jack would have been far too quick. He had other ideas. 'Very well,' he said. 'Since I can't hang you both for your silence, you'll receive fifty lashes each. The sentence is to be carried out immediately.'

The cat o'nine tales was the official whip of the British navy. It was made out of a broom handle about two feet long, the handle bound with red baize. Nine knotted strands of rope, another three feet in length, hung from the end. A dozen lashes with the cat were enough to take all the skin from a man's back. Twenty-five strokes and the deck would be slippery with blood. Fifty could kill — but once again Jack was determined that it wouldn't kill him.

22

He took the punishment gasping with pain. Mason was used to being flooged and endured the lashes in silence. At last it was over. Pails of sea-water were thrown over their raw and bleeding backs. Then they were taken back down to the cells and locked up.

'Why didn't you tell them it was Mason's picklock?' Pat asked that night as the ship groaned and creaked, still in the grip of the calm.

There was a pause. 'Because I need him alive,' Jack muttered.

Another week passed. Still the wind refused to rise. Water was cut again, and another two convicts died. The heat in the cells was stifling. The stink was almost unendurable. Nobody spoke any more. Even the effort of talking was more than anyone had strength for.

Then Anderson summoned Jack again.

The captain was drinking a glass of water as Jack was led into his cabin. He held it up so that the prisoner could see it. Jack's mouth was as dry as old leather. His lips were cracked. His back was still a mass of cuts and bruises.

'How are you feeling, Forty-one?' Anderson asked.

Jack made no answer.

'Uncommon hot isn't it?' Anderson sipped water and smiled.

'Yes, sir.' Jack's eyes were fixed on the water.

'Good.' Anderson finished the water and refilled the glass. Then he set it down on a table a few inches away from Jack. Jack stared at it. Anderson watched him carefully. A month in the cable tier and then a savage beating had had just the effect he wanted. Jack Vincent's spirit had been smashed. He was like a dog looking for a new master.

'Go on,' Anderson urged him. 'There's water there. Why don't you drink it?'

Slowly, timidly, Jack's hand stretched out. It was more water than he had seen in days. His fingers touched the edge of the glass. It felt cool. But then Anderson's hand lashed out, sweeping the glass off the table. It hit the floor and smashed. The precious water drained through the cracks.

Jack tried to speak. Instead, tears sprang to his eyes. He dropped on to his knees, his hands fumbling vaguely at the disappearing puddle of water. Anderson stood up. His eyes were alight, his face flushed with triumph.

'Mr Flack!' he called out.

The door opened. 'Yes, sir?'

'I'm making Forty-one my cabin boy,' Anderson said.

Mr Flack looked at the man who was still grovelling on the floor, tears streaming from his eyes. He felt sick inside. 'Your cabin boy, sir?' he asked.

'Yes, Mr Flack — cabin boy. He'll swab out, bring my food, wash my clothes, fetch and carry for me and keep this cabin spotless. Won't you Forty-one?'

'Yes, sir.' Jack's voice was hardly more than a whimper.

'You don't want to spend another month in the dark, do you?' Anderson gloated.

Jack shook his head. Tears pattered on to the wooden floor. The man was broken, there could be no doubt of it.

He had come on to the ship an adventurer. Now he was no more than a slave.

24

2

In the days that followed, Jack was kept busy
washing, carrying and generally waiting on Captain Anderson. He would bring in his evening
meal and watch him eat it, occasionally devour-
ing the small scraps that were thrown his way.
He would polish the officer's boots until he could
see his own servile, twitching face reflected in the
leather. He would spend hours alone in Anderson's cabin, dusting and polishing or perhaps
rearranging the maps that cluttered up the
captain's desk.

At first the crew couldn't believe that such an
arrogant man could have been humbled in this
way. Then, when it was obvious that Jack really
had become a mere cabin boy, they laughed at
him, tripping him up as he hurried along the
decks. Eventually they forgot all about him. The
wind had risen again. The *Success* was ploughing
forward. According to the captain, Norfolk
Island was less than a week away.

In fact they were only four days from their destination when Harry Anderson realized that he
had made a fatal mistake.

He was on the deck talking to Towers, the surgeon, when he turned round to tell Jack to fetch
some water. But Jack wasn't there.

'Where the devil's he got to?' he demanded. 'Forty-one!' There was no reply. And yet he hadn't given his cabin boy permission to leave. He should have been standing there, waiting for his master's commands. 'Forty-one!' he called again, louder this time. Nothing. A slow smile spread across Anderson's face. It was just what he needed to celebrate the end of the long voyage. Vincent had stepped out of line. 'By Heaven, I'll make you skip!' he muttered to himself.

Leaving Towers, he strode along the deck and back to his cabin. He pushed open the door with the palm of his hand, not even breaking his stride as he marched in. The cabin seemed empty. Where was Vincent? Then the door slammed shut behind him. He turned just in time to see a fist come crashing into the side of his jaw. Staggering back, he collapsed against the desk, finally slumping on to the floor. He felt a hand pull the sword out of his belt. And then he was looking up four feet of sharpened steel at the face of the man who held it.

'Get up!' Jack Vincent commanded.

And that was when Anderson realized his mistake. He thought he had broken Vincent, but it had all been a pretence. It was no slave who stood here now, but the old, arrogant Vincent that he both envied and loathed. Anderson had been fooled. He had let Vincent out of his cell. And now it was Vincent who was the master of the situation.

'You'll hang for this!' Anderson promised.

'Maybe.' Jack held out one hand. 'Your keys!'

Anderson opened his mouth to call out, but at once the sword was pressed against his throat, the point pricking his skin and drawing blood.

'If you make a sound, Harry, I'll kill you,' Jack said. 'Now — first I want the keys. Then I want you to sit quietly with your hands behind your back.'

Minutes later, Anderson was tightly bound, a coil of rope looping from his wrists to his neck. 'You've signed your own death warrant, Vincent!' he snarled, struggling on the floor.

'Keep your mouth shut if you want to stay alive, Harry.'

'I'm going to stay alive,' Anderson hissed. 'I don't intend to miss your execution.'

Jack ignored him. His cabin-boy act had served him well and in the past few days he'd had plenty of opportunity to search the captain's cabin, studying his maps and checking his keys against the lockers. Now he removed a key from the desk and opened an adjacent locker. When he turned round, he was holding a pistol, which he pointed at Anderson's head.

'Call the bosun,' Jack demanded.

Anderson sat hunched up on the floor, tight-lipped and defiant.

Jack pressed the barrel of the gun against the captain's ear, the cold metal pressing into the lobe. 'Don't lose your head, Harry,' he said.

The words were spoken softly, reasonably. Somehow that made them all the more deadly. A bead of sweat trickled down Anderson's forehead. He took a deep breath. 'Bosun!' he called.

As ever, Mr Flack responded quickly to the call. But this time he had no sooner opened the door than he felt his collar grabbed and suddenly he was being propelled into the room. Jack kicked the door shut and advanced on the unfortunate man who was staring first at the captain then at

27

him as if he was watching some incredible magic trick.

Jack nodded towards Anderson. 'Gag him!' he said.

The boatswain hesitated for a moment. But he remembered what Jack had been through on board the *Success* and didn't like to think what the convict might do if he was angered further. With a muttered, 'Sorry, sir,' under his breath, he pulled off Anderson's stocking and then rammed it into the captain's mouth. He was just tightening it when he felt the gun against the back of his neck.

'The keys,' Jack said.

'No . . .'

'Yes . . .'

It was the last thing Mr Flack heard. The butt of the gun crashed down on the back of his head and he fell, sprawling across the captain.

Jack took the keys and tucked the gun into the belt of his trousers, hiding it under his shirt. Then with a last look at the two men, lying on the floor in a clumsy embrace, he left the cabin. Once again, Anderson had played right into his hands. A few weeks before, the sight of a convict walking freely across the decks would have been unthinkable. But the crew was used to him. He was just the cabin boy, off on another errand. Nobody tried to stop him as he made his way down to the cells. Nobody even gave him a second glance.

Fifteen convicts had died from the flux in the course of the crossing, but there were still twenty-seven of them in the cells. Jack started with Mason, opening the cell door and thrusting the keys into his hands.

'Let 'em all out, Mason,' he said. 'We're taking over the ship.'

Mason gazed at Jack in astonishment. He had been just as fooled as Anderson and Mr Flack. But the keys and the determined look in Jack's face told their own story. Forgetting their old feud, forgetting everything in the excitement of the moment, he hurried off and began unlocking the cells.

'What the devil are you up to?' Pat was one of the first convicts out. He seemed almost unwilling to go.

'What does it look like?' Jack replied. He looked about him. 'Mason!' The old gun captain pushed his way through the milling crowd of convicts. 'Take two men to the armoury,' Jack went on. 'Break out the muskets!'

'I'll do that.' An ugly smile spread across Mason's face.

Jack grabbed him by the arm. 'There's to be no killing.'

'That's what you think.'

Mason tried to break free, but Jack still held him tightly. 'I'll make this short, Mason!' he snarled. 'I don't give a damn what you think of me, but I saved your life and took fifty lashes for it. No killing. Understand?'

For a moment it looked as if Mason was going to fight. Whatever the circumstances, he didn't like Jack and he didn't trust him. But nor could he argue with him. 'No killing,' he muttered, then turned away and made for the fore powder magazine where the guns were stored.

Jack's timing had been perfect. With land so close, the crew was relaxed, the officers unwary. Only one sailor even saw the convicts as they crept through the ship on the way to the guns and he was unconscious on his back before he could even open his mouth to raise the alarm. Once again it was Mason who saw to the magazine's lock. His nimble fingers had only to twitch and the door was open. Then the muskets were peeled away from the wall, passing into hands that seized them eagerly, loading them with practised ease. And the muskets had a strange effect on the men. They had been pale and exhausted after the long voyage, but suddenly they were filled with new strength as if, after being treated like animals for so long, they had discovered their humanity again.

It was a bloodless mutiny. The officers didn't even know that a mutiny had taken place until they found themselves surrounded. And the crew, seeing their officers taken, could only give in gracelessly to the mutineers.

One hour before, Jack Vincent had been Convict Forty-one, a man with no name on his way to a place with no future. Now he was the captain of HMS *Success*.

Later that evening, Jack went down to visit Anderson. There had been a few reversals on the convict ship. It was the officers who were now locked up in the cells while the prisoners enjoyed the comforts of the cabins. Most of the crew had chosen to stay with their officers — the penalty for mutiny was death — and were now locked up with them. But a few, including six men who had been press-ganged, had thrown in their lot with Jack.

'Good evening, Lieutenant.' Jack smiled at Anderson through the bars of his cage. 'I trust you're not finding your new quarters too cramped.'

Anderson smiled back, refusing to rise to the bait. 'You can't sail this ship with that rabble and you know it,' he said.

'Can't I? There are plenty of seamen in "that rabble". And we're only about three hundred miles west of Norfolk Island.' Jack laughed, seeing the surprise on Anderson's face. 'Oh yes, Harry,' he explained. 'The cabin boy's been looking over your shoulder.'

'I underestimated you.' Anderson nodded slowly. 'Where will you make for?'

'That's my business.'

'What about me?'

Jack looked thoughtfully at his enemy. 'What about you, Harry?' he mused. 'You're hardly the life and soul of the party, are you?'

'Murder. Is that it?' Anderson demanded.

'No. But a chance to find out if you're as good a seaman as you think you are. I'm putting you to sea.'

'The long-boat?'

'Exactly.'

'Like Bligh,' Anderson said, recalling the mutiny on the *Bounty* that had so appalled the nation a few years before.

'Just like Bligh,' Vincent agreed. 'Only you haven't so far to go.'

'William Bligh is now Governor of New South Wales,' Anderson muttered. 'Twelve of the mutineers have been captured, and three have been hanged.'

Jack turned away, ignoring him. 'You're a mine of useless information aren't you?' he said.

The next day, Anderson was launched on his three-hundred-mile voyage. He didn't sail alone. Mr Flack, Towers, the surgeon, a junior officer by the name of Hoskins, and five sailors had chosen to go with him rather than trust their fortunes (and their necks) to Jack and his crew. For his part, Jack had given them a twenty-eight-gallon water barrel and about eighty pounds of ship's biscuits carefully wrapped in the ship's Union Jack, — only just enough to cover the journey even if it was plain sailing all the way. In addition he allowed them two muskets, a bag of shot and a small barrel of powder. As he remarked to Mason, if things got really bad, they could always use the guns on each other.

'If you miss Norfolk Island, you'll find New Zealand about five hundred miles further south,' he called out, as Anderson and the others bobbed on the surface of the ocean in their tiny boat.

The convicts roared with laughter. But Anderson was defiant. 'I'll find you, Vincent,' he promised. 'However long it takes — I'll find you.'

Jack pointed at the sea, stretching to the horizon in every direction. 'That's no duck pond, Harry.'

'Wherever you go, I'm coming after you.'

'I'd save your breath to whistle up a wind.'

'Wherever you go, Vincent . . .'

But already the long-boat had drifted away from the *Success*. Anderson shouted at Vincent. Vincent shouted at Anderson. But the wind cared nothing of their feud. It grabbed the words and pulled them away. The waves drowned out the noise. And soon Anderson was only a tiny figure lost in the great emptiness of the ocean, cursing the very sky itself.

'I'll find you, Vincent! Even if I have to search every island in the Pacific!'

Jack Vincent was free. But his problems were only beginning.

Anderson had called his crew 'rabble' and despite everything Jack had to admit that the lieutenant was right. The sailors who had come over to his side were the grumblers, the idle troublemakers that you find on every ship. The press-ganged conscripts wanted only to go home and weren't prepared to do any work to get there. As for the other convicts, most of them would throw Jack over the side if it suited them and to hell with the fact that but for him they would still be in chains. They were loyal only to themselves.

And even Jack's two right-hand men were less than ideal. Pat was too young and too timid to be of much use. And as for Mason, he made it clear with every word and gesture that he hadn't forgotten his old score with the commander of the *Cassandra*. There was an alliance between the two of them but it was an uneasy one. If Jack got into trouble, he'd have to think twice before calling on Mason to pull him out.

The first problem that he faced two days after he had set Anderson adrift was simple. What did he do now? Obviously he couldn't go back to England. His feet would no sooner touch the ground than they would be removed to dangle in mid-air; the sentence for returning was always the gallows. So where else could he go? That afternoon he talked it over with Pat and Mason in Anderson's cabin.

'We've a choice,' he said, unrolling a map. 'Stay in the Pacific or cross it.'

33

'Cross it?' Pat's eyes widened. 'Where to?'

'The Americas.'

Mason squinted at the map. 'Cross the Pacific?' he muttered.

'Look,' Jack pointed. 'We make for Fiji. From there to Samoa. Then turn north to the Hawaiians. And finally the long haul to California or Mexico.'

Mason shook his head. 'You're crazy.'

'Four months. Maybe less.' Jack shrugged. 'Where else can we make for? Do you fancy New South Wales?'

'So what do we do in America?'

'We've a ship — and a crew.'

Mason laughed bitterly. 'You call that lot a crew?'

'No,' Jack said. 'But I'll make them into one.'

There was a cold ferocity in his words that made Mason look twice. Even Pat glanced up. He had heard that voice before. 'You're another Anderson!' Mason exclaimed.

Jack gripped the side of the table, trying to keep his temper under control. He knew that there were only two men on the boat that he could trust and they were both in the room now. Mason might dislike him. He might even want to kill him, but until they were safely on land, the old sailor would stand by him.

'Listen,' he said. 'If we're to survive, we've got to have discipline. You know that, and so do the other seamen. We've got to lick the rest of them into shape . . . keep them busy, run them off their feet.

'Any trouble, we can jump on it. Hard. You ran the best gun deck in the navy, Mason — before you decided to use your other talents to get you

34

into this mess. Help me. Turn these convicts into seamen. Because if we don't, if they run riot, we're finished. All of us.'

They were brave words, but already they were spoken too late. Even as Jack, Mason and Pat studied the map, plotting their course for America, the convicts were celebrating their new-found freedom with an exhilaration that bordered on madness. The *Success*, like every other navy ship, carried a supply of rum. The convicts had found it.

And now they cut the barrels free, rolled them down the passageways, dropped them with a crash down the hatchways. One of the convicts had found an axe. He swung it. The wood splintered and there was a great roar as the dark brown liquid spilled out. At once the convicts crowded round like flies at a picnic. Tin mugs and wooden goblets appeared out of nowhere to be filled, emptied and refilled, again and again.

'To freedom, boys!' one of them shouted.

A second barrel fell. Rum surged across the floor. Another convict crouched on his hands and knees like a dog, lapping it up, his tongue rasping against the wooden planks. Someone was singing. More barrels were brought out and broached.

They were still drinking an hour later when the storm hit them.

It sprang up out of nowhere. First the wind came, punching and jabbing at the sails. The waves seemed to sharpen, cutting at the sides of the boat like a thousand metal scythes. Then the clouds rolled in, forming an impenetrable barrier that blotted out the sun and locked the *Success* in a swelling darkness. The thunder tried to break in, pounding against the clouds with invisible fists. Cracks appeared, brilliant silver against the ugly black sky. The ship began to turn — now one way now another, out of control.

Jack was at the wheel, fighting with it, trying to move the rudder through a suddenly reluctant sea. 'The wind's stiffening!' he called out. 'Get 'em aloft, Mason. Reef the topsails.'

'Reef the topsails!' Mason shouted.

Then a door opened and two convicts staggered on to the deck. For perhaps half a second Jack thought it was the pitching and the tossing of the boat that was to blame. But then with a hollow feeling he saw the truth. Both men were drunk. He opened his mouth to speak but the words were obliterated by a seering, splintering crash as another fork of lightning ripped its way down to the sea.

'Glory be!' Pat whispered. 'They've broached the grog.'

'Take the wheel,' Jack commanded.

'What me?' The colour drained out of Pat's face. 'But I never . . .'

'Now's your chance to learn!'

Leaving Pat in an unwilling dance with the steering wheel, Jack leapt down and grabbed hold of one of the convicts hoping to shake some sense into the man. But even from a distance, as the stink of rum carried itself to his nostrils, he knew it was hopeless. The door opened again and Mason appeared. He had been below deck. Now, seeing Jack, he shook his head.

'There's not one of 'em fit for anything,' he shouted above the roar of the wind and the racing waves.

36

Jack looked over his shoulder, his black hair flapping about his head. 'We'll run before it,' he shouted back. But the wind was blowing even harder. It was howling across the deck and his words were lost in the din.

The waves rose. It was impossible to tell where they ended and the clouds began. All the colours in the world seemed to have mixed together like spilled paint and everything was a dirty green. Now the *Success* was flying, climbing slowly up one great mountain and then hurling itself off the top. Down in the hold, the convicts fell back in terror as the remaining barrels tore themselves free and shattered against the walls. Sea water poured in from all sides, hammering them to their knees and spinning them helplessly down the corridors. Screaming, blind with panic, they tried to reach the ladders that led to the hatchways and the decks. But it was too late. The water was coming in too fast. Half of them were drowned in the very cells that had brought them there.

And still the storm worsened. Mason had taken over at the wheel lashing himself to the spokes with a coil of rope that he had snatched up from the deck. Pat was at his feet, his eyes closed, moaning with terror. The night had come in uninvited on the day. Although it was only early afternoon, the blackness was total, interrupted only by the lightning that flickered briefly above the mayhem.

It was the wind that finished it. It swung across the ocean, a battering ram that found its target in the heart of the *Success*. Jack felt the deck vanish underneath his feet. For a moment he thought he was floating in mid-air. Then he hit the wood again, the rough planks tearing clothes

37

and skin alike. He tried to open his eyes but he was blinded by the stinging, icy spray. He called out to Mason but there was no answer. Forcing his eyes open, one hand across his face to protect them, he searched through the swirling chaos for the steering wheel. It was spinning free. There was no sign of Mason or Pat.

If his eyes had been shut then he would have died. He just had time to see a towering shape plunge down towards him in a hideous tangle of rope and canvas. The main mast had been torn free. He was directly in its path. He got up and threw himself backwards, all in one movement. His shoulders cleared the side of the boat. Then there was nothing until he hit the sea far below, breaking through the surface and plunging into a dark and silent oblivion.

Cold.

Cold sand. In his eyes. In his mouth.

Bruises. His whole body felt broken. He twitched his fingers, then kicked with his feet, and was surprised to find that they still worked.

Jack Vincent opened his eyes. The storm had settled. The light was fading at the end of the day so he must have been unconscious for several hours. Unless this was the dawn of the following day and he had lain there the whole night.

Lain where?

He was on a beach. A line of palm trees stood in a tapering curve opposite the sea. The sand looked grey, but perhaps that was just the light. A few boxes floated in the shallows, surrounded by wreckage. The body of a convict lay, face down in the water, his hands stretched out as if in one last, futile attempt to grab hold of the shore.

38

Jack got slowly to his feet. Then he was sick.

Later, much later, he walked away, following the shore. He had no idea where he was going. Perhaps he would find other survivors. Perhaps something useful would have been washed up from the *Success*. Even the rum, which had been so largely responsible for the catastrophe, would have been welcome now.

He walked for almost half a mile before he heard voices. Ahead of him, glowing red behind a sand dune, he could see the light of a fire.

'Cannibals,' the first voice growled. It was a pessimistic voice. 'I've heard they're all over the Pacific. Let's hope there ain't any around here!'

'And me preparing for sleep!' The second voice was high-pitched and indignant. There could be no mistaking the Irish accent. 'A fine time to tell me I'm likely to be eaten!'

Jack stepped forward, climbing over the dune. There was a bonfire on the other side, the flames crackling against a starlit sky. Sure enough there were two men crouched in front of it. As they heard him approach, one of them spun round, gripping a knife.

'Vincent!' Mason exclaimed.'

'Holy Mother . . .' Pat began.

Jack smiled. 'Hello, boys,' he said.

3

Pat and Mason were cooking a few small fish over a fire lit from the flint sparks of a pistol. Jack was trimming saplings with a knife saved from the wreckage. It was the evening of the next day and by now they knew that they were the only three to survive the destruction of the *Success*. But for how long? The fish that they had managed to catch were tough and boney ... barely enough for one. They had to find food. They had to find shelter. And they had to do it soon.

'Ugh!' Mason had taken a mouthful of fish. He chewed it with a look of disgust. 'Gives you the gut ache.'

'We'll do better tomorrow.' Jack bent the sapling into a sort of hoop and bound the ends with a strip of creeper. 'We can snare birds and make fish spears,' he said.

'And build ourselves somewhere to live,' Pat added.

'Live!' Mason spat. 'You got us in a proper mess, Vincent. We'd have been a long sight better off if we *had* reached Norfolk Island.'

Mason was not in a good mood. It often seemed that Mason was never in a good mood. They argued again that evening — this time about whose turn it was to take the watch. Mason lost.

As well as the knife, they had managed to salvage one pistol from the ship and this never left their sight. Mason's stories of cannibals hung in the air like a bad smell. More than once Pat had said he thought he was being watched. So while he and Jack slept, Mason kept the gun. He just hoped he wouldn't need to use it.

In the morning, the gun was gone, and the knife with it.

It was Jack who found Mason, fast asleep at his post. It would have been a court martial offence in the navy, but out here, on an island in the middle of nowhere, Jack simply shrugged it off. They were still alive. That was all that mattered.

Then Mason discovered the theft. 'You've swiped them!' he said. 'You thieving Irish tinker!'

'Swiped what?' Pat looked up with large, innocent eyes.

'My pistol and my knife.' Mason was frantically running his thumbs round his belt, his eyes searching the beach. 'I'll cut the tripes from you,' he roared.

He was about to hurl himself on the cowering Irishman but Jack stopped him. 'Hold hard, Mason!' he said. 'What would he want to do that for?'

'That's right!' Pat was crouching on all fours, ready to bolt. 'What would I want to do that for?'

'Well, if he didn't take it . . .' Mason began.

'That's right.' Jack nodded grimly. 'We're not alone on this island.'

They began the search the same day, keeping close to the sea for fear of losing themselves in the thick woodland that stretched over the hills, woodland that seemed to sprout and grow even as they

41

watched. The trees were like none Jack had ever seen, the trunks twisted into elaborate knots and the leaves exploding in all shapes and sizes like green fireworks. The climate was hot, but it was a pleasant dry heat that carried the scent of timber and flowers.

With a clear blue sea on their left, the three men pressed forward. They hardly spoke, keeping their ears open for any sound that might warn them of an attack. They were not alone on the island. And they were unarmed. It wasn't a very comforting thought.

They had walked for about two miles, exploring every bay and inlet before they came upon another human being. Jack saw him first and raised a warning hand. Pat and Mason stopped behind him and stared over his shoulder, Mason's eyes drawn to the knife that the figure held in his hand. It was his knife.

The figure was a young man of about eighteen. He was a native of the island, dressed only in a roughly woven skirt bound around his waist. He had a lithe, athletic body, the muscles clearly defined beneath his dark skin. His hair was a mass of curls. Swirling lines decorated his face which was now fixed in concentration. He was working on a canoe. One whole side had been broken in and he was using Mason's knife to cut away the splintered wood, obviously enjoying the extra strength that the sharpened blade gave him.

One step at a time, Jack moved forward. He wasn't even sure quite what he was going to do, but if the youth had Mason's knife he might also have the gun, and Jack didn't intend letting that go. But when he was about ten feet away the youth must have heard or sensed him. He looked up from his work, fear in his eyes. At the same moment, Jack leapt.

The two of them rolled over in the sand, the knife flying into the air. Although he was only half Jack's size, the young man was strong and as slippery as an eel. Wrenching his arms, he broke free and would have got away altogether if Pat hadn't thrown himself on him too. Meanwhile, Mason had retrieved the knife. As Jack struggled on the sand, he saw him approach, saw the look of murder in his eyes. Leaving the youth to Pat, he got to his feet, just in time to stop the sailor stabbing down. In fact the knife only missed his own throat by inches. Mason was so angry he didn't care who he killed.

'Damn you, Vincent!' he shouted, trying to free his wrist from Jack's grip. 'Get out of my way!'

'No, Mason!' Jack replied.

It looked as if the two men were going to fight it out then and there. But suddenly another voice, deep and resonant, called to them from the sea.

'E Maru!'

They turned. And froze.

A canoe ten times the size of the one on the beach had appeared out of thin air, skimming over the waves towards them. There was no time to move, no time to do anything. Even as Jack watched, it leapt forward with incredible speed, covering the last few years in seconds. Twenty or more warriors crouched in two lines inside it, each holding a single oar, pounding rhythmically at the water. A face had been painted on the bow with glaring eyes and grimacing mouth. The stern, rising vertically above the surface of the sea, could have been a tail. The whole thing had been designed to resemble a sea-serpent and now it hissed as it slid over the sand, the warriors leaping out. Jack, Mason and Pat were surrounded. The youth rolled free.

A man moved forward and embraced him. He was older than the rest, dressed in a cloak of brightly-coloured feathers. He was the chief. Jack could tell that even without understanding a word that he was saying — for he was talking all the while, seemingly questioning the youth that they had just attacked. Attacked? Jack's stomach turned. If the youth was the chief's son and the old man assumed they'd been trying to kill him, their own future wouldn't be too bright. He glanced to one side and saw that Pat was whispering — the Lord's prayer. The same thought had obviously just occurred to him.

Then the young man said something and the chief's face changed. From concern and affection he showed only anger. He pushed the youth away, then slapped his face. The youth muttered something. The chief gave an order.

'That's it . . .' Mason muttered.

The circle of warriors closed in on the three castaways, hands reaching out to take them.

The village was on the other side of the island, hidden behind a volcano that soared elegantly over the forests. At first sight the houses were more roof than anything else. There were about ten of them, forming a rough semi-circle around a clearing and facing the sea. Each roof was made from some sort of straw, slanting down like an improbable hat on four thick wooden poles. The roof came down so low that you had to crouch to go through the door which was only a few feet high. Inside, too, it was difficult to stand fully upright — not that this mattered to Pat, Mason and Jack who were sitting squat, securely tied up and unable to stand at all.

At least they were still alive, but this did not seem to cheer Mason. 'There's a curse on you, Jack Vincent,' he growled. 'I should've cut the heart from you a long time ago.'

He fell silent as a figure appeared in the doorway. It was the young man who had been the cause of their trouble in the first place. Slowly, he moved into the house and stood over Jack, staring at him curiously. Then he pointed.

'You . . . captain?' he asked.

Jack was so surprised to hear English words coming from the young man that for a moment he just sat there blinking. Then he nodded his head. The youth smiled and produced the stolen knife. Pat flinched. But to their relief the youth cut through their bonds and motioned at them to follow him.

The light was beginning to fade, pink stains blotting the sky, as they were led through the village, feeling rather like exotic animals. There must have been more than fifty people in the area. The women, naked to the waist, pointed and giggled at them. The children, who wore no clothes at all, stared and kept a safe distance. And the men, some of whom had been in the canoe, stood watching them gravely, their faces hostile and arrogant.

The youth seemed to be in control, which confirmed Jack's belief that he was the son of the chief. He muttered a couple of words and two warriors sprang forward to guard the prisoners.

Under this escort they were led into the centre of the village and forced to sit on the ground in front of a huge bonfire.

'Dinner time . . .' Pat whispered.

'Yes.' Mason sniffed. 'Let's hope we ain't *it*.'

But it appeared that the young man had other plans for them. As the three men sat waiting, a group of villagers walked into the clearing carrying baskets laden high with roasted meat, fresh fish, bread and fruit. A young woman with a basket of vegetables crouched beside Pat and gazed into his eyes. Then, laughing, she pulled a white turnip out of the basket and pointed first at it, then at him.

'Pakeha,' she said, and the other women laughed.

Pakeha. White man. It was the first word of Maori they had learnt.

As the sun set behind the volcano and the sea shimmered silver beneath the moon, the feast began. The natives had food in abundance. No sooner was one basket empty than another was brought out. They drank only water, stored in calabashes — types of gourd — but as the evening turned to night and the night scattered its stars across the sky, a sort of intoxication set in. Some of the women sang while others danced, moving in time to the music. Finally Pat surprised everyone by leaping to his feet and dancing a jig, much to the delight of the Maoris who cheered him on.

A feast under the stars with a friendly, generous people. After the horror of the shipwreck it seemed too good to be true, and despite everything, Jack couldn't relax. The young man, the chief's son, was still staring at them. Throughout the entire evening his eyes had never left them. He wanted something, that much was clear. Jack suspected that they were only alive because of him.

But what did he want? And when the time came, would they be able to pay the price?

Another week passed before they found out. In that time, they were entertained by the Maoris as unwilling guests. It was a party they were forbidden to leave, for there were always at least two warriors with them, armed with curving clubs that also doubled as spears. But neither Pat nor Mason were complaining. For Mason it was all one long holiday, a chance to do a bit of sunbathing and to gorge himself until all he could do was sleep. Pat too was enjoying himself. The Maori girls seemed fascinated by his fair hair, and his Irish jig had made him something of a hero with them. Only Jack was watchful. He had seen where the natives kept their canoes. And feasts or no feasts, he only needed to be given one opportunity and he would be off.

They were sitting one morning in the sunlight when the chief's son approached them. They had learnt now that his name was Maru and that he was indeed eighteen years old. Having overheard Mason's angry words on the beach, he was now convinced that Mason was called 'Tripe' and Pat was called 'Tinker', and it was by these names that he now addressed them.

'You — Tripe! And you — Tinker! Go with Makiwi.' He pointed at another young warrior who stood nearby.

Mason didn't move. 'What's he talking about?' he demanded.

'Do as he says,' Jack suggested.

'Take orders from a poxy black man?' Mason rolled over on his side. 'I'll see him in hell first.'

Jack shook his head, expecting trouble, and a moment later it came. He had been observing these Maoris. They could be all smiles and welcoming gestures. But they were also ferocious. At heart they were warriors, killers. They weren't the sort of people who took no for an answer.

Maru stepped forward and reached down. One hand grabbed Mason's hair and suddenly he pulled, jerking the sailor on to his feet. Mason opened his mouth to protest but seeing the look in Maru's eyes, as well as the second warrior who was hovering close by, he raised his hands in surrender. Then, rubbing his hair, grateful that it was still fixed to his head, he walked off. Pat went too.

Maru was delighted. 'My . . . mine. My slaves!' he crowed. 'My slaves!'

And that was just what they were, Jack realized. The Maoris had been kind to them in the same way that he might have been kind to a horse or a dog. They would never leave the village. After the softening up would come the work. They would work there until they died. Slaves.

'Give me your tongue!' Maru said.

Jack stared at the young warrior, screwing his face up in puzzlement to show his lack of understanding.

'You will speak me more English,' Maru explained, stumbling over each word.

'You want me to teach you English?' It was the last thing Jack had expected.

'Teach. Teach. Teach Maru English.'

And in the weeks that followed, Jack did just

that. The youth was incredibly fast, picking up and remembering words almost immediately. Soon his broken phrases had become whole sentences and the sentences steadily more fluent. At the same time Jack learnt much about the Maori way of life, although his lessons were often painful.

On one occasion, for example, he was fishing with Maru. They had been out in the boat for about ten minutes when Jack felt a tug on his line and landed a four-pound flounder. Deftly he had knocked it on the head and thrown it into the boat, only to fall flat on his back as Maru did much the same to him.

'You idiot!' Maru screamed. 'Why do you do things so stupidly?'

'What . . .?'

'You stupid, stupid pakeha!'

Maru had sulked for the rest of the afternoon and it had taken all Jack's tact and patience to find out why. Apparently the first fish was reserved for Tangaroa, the Maori god of the sea . . . and Jack should have thrown it back. The fact that they then proceeded to catch another dozen flounders almost one after the other proved that the god couldn't have been all that displeased, but it had still cost Jack a bruised chin.

Gradually, though, the two of them became friends and as Maru's English improved, he used it to tell Jack of the gods and goddesses who, according to the Maoris, ruled over their lives. There was Rangi, the god of the sky, who married Papa, or the earth and so gave birth to the wind and the trees. Rangi and Papa had been so much in love that they had clutched each other in an

49

eternal embrace, and everything had been dark.

'The children get tired of the dark,' Maru explained. 'So they fight Rangi. They push him up. They push him higher and higher and the light comes between. Everywhere is light.' That was how the sky and the earth had been separated. And the story went on. 'When it rains, it is Rangi crying for Papa. When morning mist comes it is Papa sighing for Rangi.'

Jack smiled. It wasn't exactly what he had been taught in the Bible, but he was wise enough not to argue with Maru's version.

Mason unfortunately wasn't.

He and Pat had been having a very different time on the island. While Pat had flirted with the young girls, learning such useful Maori words as lips and eyes (nga nutu and nga kanohi), Mason had become more sullen and withdrawn by the day. The holiday was over as far as he was concerned, and had been from the moment he had discovered that the Maoris thought of him as a slave. It was inevitable that he and Maru would eventually come to blows. It finally happened one day as Maru recounted the stories of his gods.

'Rangi? Papa?' Mason had a way of sneering his words that turned them into insults. 'Heathen rubbish!' He spat on the ground just in case Maru hadn't got the message.

At once Maru was up on his feet. 'You tuati pakeha!' he exclaimed. 'White dirt!'

'What?' Now Mason was on his own feet, his fists clenched.

Maru spat back at him. 'Tuati pakeha!'

And before Jack could stop them, the two were at each other's throats, punching and kicking like sailors in a tap-room brawl. Mason was the heavier and the stronger of the two. But Maru was the more nimble, giving as good as he got and blackening one of Mason's eyes even as he was thrown on to his back on the sand.

'Stop it!' Jack shouted, trying to pull them apart. But neither of them heard him and a moment later his worst fears were realized as the old chief and about ten warriors came charging across the clearing towards them. The chief — his name was Tahuru — was holding a club, and without breaking his stride he used it to pummel the two fighters, not caring which one got the worst of it. His face was filled with anger. Eventually Maru and Mason rolled apart and lay panting in the sand.

'Tamariki porangi!' the chief yelled, shaking the club. 'Piipii tiko!'

Jack didn't understand a word of it, but it was enough to know that Tahuru was furious. His harangue went on for another five minutes before he turned on his heel and marched back to his hut. Mason got up, rubbing his eye and smiling as if he'd just done something clever. Jack looked at Maru thoughtfully.

There was nothing to smile about, he knew. Somehow Maru had persuaded the chief to spare the pakehas in the first place. They were tolerated only as Maru's slaves. But slaves didn't lounge about in the sun doing nothing. Slaves certainly didn't fight with their masters.

Maru was losing control. And without him they were dead.

Maru had realized this too, and a few days later he sought out Jack as he sat with Mason in the shadow of a palm tree.

51

'Ngati Miru . . .' he began.

Jack had heard the name before. It was the name of a tribe who lived on the other side of the volcano. Maru's tribe had been at war with them for generations. Nobody could even remember quite how the war had begun. It was simply there, a fact of life, to be fought until one or the other of them had been annihilated.

'My father . . .' Maru continued. 'He is our rangatira . . .'

'Rangatira?'

'Our chief. But they know him. Ngati Miru know our tricks. Now we need new ones. You, Jack — you will help us.'

Jack shook his head. 'Wait a minute . . .'

But Maru was determined and Jack understood why. He had lost face with his own people. The three white men had been nothing but trouble. So Maru planned to use them, to show that his slaves really could be worth something.

'A ship is coming,' Maru explained. 'We will buy muskets. You will teach us to use them. We will go to war. Shot will be too fast for the Ngati Miru. They go. No more trouble for us.'

Maru nodded and moved away. As soon as he had gone, Mason, who had been sitting through all this with his eyes closed as if asleep, sat up and sniffed, a slow smile spreading across his lips. 'There ain't no ship and you know it,' he said. It's just Maru's dream, that's what. A ship? Set me dreaming too. A passage out of here . . .'

'Or a rope round your neck if it happens to be British,' Jack reminded him.

Mason shook his head. 'Bilge water, Vincent. There ain't no ship.'

That was when Pat appeared, running over the

brow of a hill, shouting and gesticulating. A second later there was a soft explosion in the distance, the sound of a cannon.

There was a ship. It had lowered its anchor. And for Jack and the others, it might be their one and only chance to escape.

4

Clouds of white smoke drifted from the bow of
the ship that sat moored in the bay on the other
side of the village. The sound of the cannon
echoed in the morning air. All the natives had run
down to the beach to greet the new arrivals, chat-
tering with excitement. Already a jolly boat had
been launched and was making for the shore, six
men pulling at the oars. The ship flew no colours.
It was a small caravel, Portuguese in origin and
developed for exploring . . . fast, light and fit for
all winds.

'Well, at least she ain't a man-o'-war,' Mason
said.

The three of them were standing some distance
away, watching the throng of villagers and the
approaching jolly boat. Now Mason moved as if
to run down the hill and join them, but Jack held
him back.

'Hold it,' he said. 'Maru isn't going to let you
just walk out of here. He has other plans for us.'

'To fight his Niggerti Miroo?' Mason spat. 'I
didn't come all this way to fight his rotten wars
for him.'

'Maybe. But it might be best to keep out of
sight until we know which way the wind blows.'

'It's not like you to be so wary.' Mason eyed

Jack curiously. 'You're usually the first into trouble.'

'First in when I know there's a way out,' Jack replied. 'Right now I'm not so sure . . .'

The captain of the caravel stepped on to dry land, his leather-booted foot grinding into the sand. The ship's name was the *Sea Wolf*. The captain was called De Witt, a fat, oily man with a small moustache and a mass of uneven stubble. When he smiled his mouth revealed more gaps than teeth, and those left were stunted and horribly yellow. His eyes were yellow too. He was dressed in clothes that had seen better days, and probably better owners. Nothing fitted and the whole outfit seemed held together by dirt.

Nonetheless, the Maoris greeted him warmly, leading him up to the village where the chief, Tahuru, was waiting to greet him. De Witt seemed equally pleased to see the old man. He seized him with bear-like hands, rubbed noses in the Maori fashion and thumped him on the back.

'How are you, you smelly old rascal?' he boomed. His eyes, which missed nothing, flickered to the knife and pistol that hung at Tahuru's waist. 'Been knocking some pakehas on the head, have you?' he demanded.

Tahuru nodded, grinning. 'Yes. Good. Very good. Mai tikana!'

De Witt drew himself up and rested his hands on his legs. Behind him the warriors had formed a circle with Maru at the centre. 'Now, you son of Satan,' he muttered confidentially, 'we get down to business, eh? But none of your double-crossing monkey-tricks . . .'

'My father's no double-crossing monkey, Captain,' Maru interrupted. 'More likely you are!'

De Witt's head snapped round. For a moment his eyes were full of suspicion but then he forced the smile back to his lips, 'Well, well!' he exclaimed. 'If it isn't young Maru! Your English has improved, hasn't it!'

'You bring muskets?' Maru demanded.

'Maybe.'

'How many?'

'How many do you want?'

Maru held up his hands and spread all his fingers out twice.

'Twenty?' De Witt whistled. 'What do I get?'

'Water, food, fish, flax,' Maru said.

'I don't want flax.'

'Then what do you want, Captain?'

'Men.' De Witt looked about him. The smile was still firmly fixed in place, but it was a strained, artificial smile. Although he had been friendly enough to Tahuru and his son, he was still surrounded by sailors who had followed him up from the jolly boat. And those sailors were all armed. 'Men,' he repeated in a low voice. 'They come aboard ship. Sail three days. Work one moon. Come back.'

Maru shook his head. 'What you say and what you do — are two islands apart.'

'You don't trust me?'

'You crazy?'

'Tell the old man . . .'

The entire conversation had been overheard by Jack, Mason and Pat who had back-tracked to their hut, only a short distance away from Tahuru's. Now they listened carefully as the bargaining went on. Tahuru refused to lend the captain any of his men, not even for a morning. There

56

was another flurry of conversation, with Maru acting as interpreter, and Tahuru made a counter offer. If De Witt lent them the muskets, they would pay him back with slaves taken in the war against the Ngati Miru. But this was unacceptable to De Witt.

'What if you lose the war?' he demanded. Where will my muskets be then? Tell me that, Maru. You're wasting my time!'

Maru translated, then waited as Tahuru let fly with a torrent of abuse. It was hard to tell, but Jack thought the chief was angrier with his son than with De Witt. A moment later he found out why.

'I have three pakehas,' Maru said. He didn't sound very happy about it. 'My slaves. You buy. Ten muskets.'

'Pakehas?' Pat whispered. 'That's us!'

'Yes,' Jack muttered. 'And I thought we were worth more than ten muskets.'

De Witt clearly didn't agree. 'White men?' he said, his voice dismissing them. 'What would I want with them? I want warriors, Tahuru. And if you want your muskets, you'll know where to find me.'

The meeting was over. De Witt joined his men and together they marched back to the jolly boat.

'What now?' Mason asked.

'Now?' Jack thought for a moment. 'You heard what he said. He needs men. Come on ... we could be just the men he needs!'

Captain De Witt strode across the sand to the jolly boat, his mind racing ahead of him. When Maru had mentioned white men he had been careful to feign complete lack of interest ... but of course, nothing could have been further from the truth. He was fascinated to know what three white men could be doing on the island, hundreds of miles from civilization. And could he use them? De Witt rubbed at his stubble with the tips of his fingers. Yes. Three pakehas would be perfect, once he'd found them. Or rather, once they'd found him.

'Captain . . .'

De Witt came to an abrupt halt. Things were working out just as he had hoped. The three men had run round from the village and were waiting at the jolly boat, fearful of being seen. Quickly, he sized them up. Their leader, young and arrogant. A boy, fast and wiry. An old sailor with no love for either of them. Just what he needed . . .

'Captain De Witt, at your service,' he said.

'Jack Vincent.' The leader pointed at the other two men. 'George Mason. Pat Cassidy.'

'How the devil's name did you get yourselves into this pickle?' De Witt asked.

'If it's not inconvenient, Captain, might we talk aboard your ship?'

De Witt smiled knowingly. 'Don't want to upset your Maori friends, eh? Well, no more do I. Get into the jolly-boat. You can hide under the bulwarks.'

It seemed that the Maoris were still arguing among themselves in the village. Nobody tried to stop Jack and the others as they slipped on to the boat and they reached the *Sea Wolf* without incident. From a distance, sitting in the sunlit bay, the ship had seemed like something out of a fairy tale. Close to it was less magical. As Jack followed De Witt to his cabin, his eyes took in the decks, filthy and unswabbed, the metal

58

stanchions, rusting and tarnished. All the paint-work was flaking and the ropes — first sign of a competent seaman — were knotted and frayed. An empty bottle rolled back and forth in the scuppers.

Mason was unconcerned. 'I can't believe it!' he muttered. 'I never thought I'd set foot on a ship's deck again.'

De Witt grabbed hold of a seaman coming sleepily out of the hold. 'Wake up, you slob!' he cried. 'Bring some grub to my cabin — fast!'

'Good honest grub!' Mason licked his lips. 'No fern roots or fish or oysters or muck like that! Captain, I'd give my life for a piece of salt pork.'

'You shall have it,' De Witt promised.

And in this, at least, he was as good as his word. While the three men ate, Jack told him how they had ended up as castaways on the island. It was a good story, a moving story. It was, how-ever, very far from being a true story. Jack, thinking it might be better not to mention that they were all three escaped convicts and muti-neers, made the whole thing up.

'So you were the only survivors?' De Witt poured himself some more rum. 'Well,' he went on, 'the customs of the Maoris being what they are, you're lucky to be alive.' He chuckled to him-self, then glanced sharply at Jack. 'Tell me, Mr Vincent, what were you trading in so far south?'

'Flax.'

'So.'

The captain held him in his glance. He knew Jack was lying. But that didn't bother him. He was more used to lies than the truth.

'And you, Captain?' Jack asked. 'You're not in flax . . .'

59

'No. We're pearlers, Mr Vincent.'

'In these parts?'

'We've had our share of bad luck — just like you.' De Witt drained his glass. 'We were boarded by pirates. They took everything and killed half the crew. We made it to Dutch Batavia and picked up more hands. But . . . well you've seen the state of the ship. Scum they were. Deserters from ships. Escaped convicts.'

The last two words hung heavy in the air. Pat, who had been drifting off to sleep after the food and drink, woke up. Mason froze with a forkful of meat halfway to his mouth. Only Jack sat impassively, waiting for the captain to go on.

'In the end I threw 'em overboard,' De Witt said. 'They tried to take over the ship, you see. A big mistake.'

'You drowned 'em?' Mason asked.

'Oh no!' The captain beamed. 'The sharks got 'em first . . .'

He stood up and went over to the door, opening it as if to let in a bit of fresh air. But Jack wasn't fooled. De Witt was making sure they weren't overheard.

'I set sail for the Horn,' he went on, 'but the winds were against us. We were blown clean off course and as I was short of provisions, I put in to the coast.'

'Which coast?' Jack asked.

'Never mind that. Let's just say I came ashore about fifty miles south of here. I wanted to fill our casks with fresh water, but while I was wading through the stream, I saw something. Gleaming, yellow specks.'

He had lowered his voice. Suddenly it was very quiet in the cabin.

'Gold!' Mason whispered.

'Gold,' De Witt agreed. 'Not much, maybe. But with a day's march into the mountains . . . who knows? The trouble is, I need men to pan the gold and get it back to the ship. But I can't trust my crew. They'd cut my throat as soon as spit in the ocean.'

'And you trust us?' Jack asked.

'I don't trust anyone,' De Witt countered. 'But I need you just like you need me and that seems good enough for a start.'

'So where do we come in?'

De Witt nodded at Jack. 'You and I hold the ship. Your two mates go into the hills with the Maoris.'

'They didn't seem too eager to help,' Jack said.

'They refused today. But tomorrow I'll put two casks of rum ashore. When the Maoris have finished that, they'll want more. "Come aboard!" we'll say. And before they've sobered up, we'll be at sea and they'll be down in the hold under battened hatches.'

De Witt laughed, a harsh, rattling sound. Jack forced a smile to his face. 'You're full of bright ideas, Captain.'

'With your help we can do it. I'll give you a share in the gold and put you ashore wherever you want. What d'you say?'

But nobody had time to say anything. A second later the door burst open and Maru appeared, his hand clutching a spear, his body dripping with sea-spray from the fast canoe-ride out to the *Sea Wolf*. Four warriors stood behind him. Their faces were angry, their eyes burning.

'You are a tricky monkey, Captain!' he jabbered at De Witt. 'And you also, Jack! If you return here, I will kill you. You stay in village. There will be no more warnings . . .!'

Mason had half-risen out of his chair but Jack pushed him back. Slowly, he lifted his glass at De Witt. They had to go back now. He knew they had no choice. But Maru had arrived too late. A bargain had been made.

It was a bargain De Witt had no intention of keeping.

Later that afternoon he was sitting in his cabin with the bosun, a small, pig-like man with a scar joining his ears across his throat like a second smile. The two men knew each other well. Well enough to be sure they never turned their backs on each another.

'You're mad, Captain,' the bosun was saying. 'We don't need three extra hands and you know it. So long as it can smell gold, the crew's loyal to a man.'

'We don't need 'em, but we can use 'em,' De Witt replied. 'Just to keep an extra eye on things. But once we've got the gold . . .'

'Aye, you'll have other plans for them.'

De Witt smiled. 'Dead men tell no tales.'

After they had been escorted back to the village, Jack, Mason and Pat had been left by themselves in their hut. But Maru was taking no chances while De Witt was still in sight. Two armed warriors crouched outside by the porch and on the one occasion when Mason had tried to leave, he had found himself threatened with a heavy greenstone cudgel — a 'mere' as the Maoris called it.

Now he was in an ugly mood. 'Soon as it gets

62

dark, we stove in the heads of them two varmints outside and skip it,' he said.

'Where to?' Jack asked.

'De Witt, of course.'

Jack shook his head. 'He won't welcome you. Not until he's got his Maoris aboard.'

'Then we'll wait. Wait until they're half-seas over.'

'And then share their fate?'

'What do you mean?' Mason squinted at Jack.

'The Maoris will never come back,' Jack said. 'De Witt wouldn't dare return after double-crossing Tahuru.'

'What of it?'

'They'll end up with the sharks, like the last crew. And where do you think that leaves us? How long will we last once De Witt's got his gold?'

Mason fell into gloomy silence. Pat bit his finger-nails. Jack drew himself up and waited. There was nothing else to be done.

De Witt had already delivered the rum according to his plan. He and five sailors, all heavily armed, had come ashore in the jolly-boat, carrying the heavy kegs with them. They had been met by a crowd of delighted Maoris and as the sun set the banquet had begun. Jack, Mason and Pat were the only ones who hadn't been invited.

Tahuru drank first. His thin arms were surprisingly strong and he had no difficulty lifting a whole barrel in front of his head. He tilted it back and the golden liquid splashed on to his lips. It was a signal for everyone else to join in. The Maoris had never tasted rum before the arrival of De Witt. They weren't used to it, making it all the more potent. Shouting and fighting they

63

scrambled for the remaining barrels, women and children jostling with the warriors in their eagerness to get a share.

Soon they were drunk. It was a wild, spinning, fiery drunkenness that made them seem more savage than ever. Some of the men came together to perform a 'haka'. This was a Maori war dance ... and often it looked more like a real war than any sort of dance. The warriors brandished their weapons. Their eyes bulged and their tongues stuck out. Shouting, they pounded at the sand with their feet. De Witt had gone back to the ship but the bosun was still there and, watching them, he felt a tremor of fear that he couldn't dismiss. He would just be glad when the Maoris were too drunk to move. Then he would select a dozen or so of the fittest, get back to the *Sea Wolf* and be fifty miles away before anyone woke up.

Back in the hut, Jack could hear the growing pandemonium. Behind him, Mason and Pat each held pieces of wood, taken from a table that they had torn apart. 'How many men are still on the ship, do you think?' he asked.

Mason thought back. 'Well, there's De Witt. And from what I saw, I'd say four others.'

'So the odds are five to three.'

'Easy!' Pat tapped the palm of his hand with a table leg. 'I've got me shillelagh ...'

Mason moved to the door. 'Dance away, you jumping jackanapes!' he yelled. 'You'll dance to another tune before the day's done.'

The Maoris were dancing themselves into a frenzy now. Night had fallen. A silver-flamed shooting star arched across the heavens and lanced down behind the volcano like a spear thrown by the hand of Rangi himself. The sky was pitch black, the stars burning brilliantly, reflected in the shimmering sea. A huge bonfire had been built in the centre of the clearing and now it writhed and twisted almost as if it were trying to join in the dance. A cool breeze came in over the waves, wrapping itself around the palm trees and snaking silently through the tall grass.

The Maoris danced. The rum poured. As each keg was broached it was carried away spinning across eager, outstretched hands. The haka had become more violent than ever. The whole village — the very volcano itself — seemed to tremble beneath the stamping feet. The bosun and his seamen looked on, smiling. But the smiles were thin. If anything went wrong they would be torn apart before they could move . . . no matter how many guns they carried.

But when things did go wrong it was in a way that nobody could have foreseen.

One of the seamen had set his musket down to light a pipe, using a splinter of wood taken out of the fire. Concentrating on the flame, he hadn't noticed one of the younger Maoris come creeping out of the shadows. But the Maori had seen the gun. He wanted it, and now he took it.

He had never held a gun before. First he looked down the barrel and was disappointed to see nothing there. He held it up, the barrel slanting over his shoulder. His finger found the trigger. He pulled it. There was an explosion and the Maori was thrown off his feet. Fortunately the gun had been pointing into the air and nobody was hurt. But the damage had already been done.

Tahuru heard the explosion. Befuddled with rum, he decided that De Witt had betrayed him and that his village was under attack. He was still carrying Mason's pistol. Drunkenly, he lifted it and fired. It was the worst thing he could have done.

The second shot, fired by their chief, persuaded the drunken Maoris that they had been tricked and fallen into an ambush. At once the dancing stopped and their weapons were snatched up to defend themselves. And yet, in truth, there was little change in their appearance. They had been ferocious to start with. They were ferocious now. Only the bosun could feel the difference. Before, the violence had been controlled, channelled into the intricate movements of the war dance. Now it was bursting out, stampeding towards him and his men.

'Back! Fall back!'

As he shouted the order, one of the Maoris rose up in front of him, his club raised. The bosun fired his musket. The warrior screamed and blood spouted from his neck. The others closed in behind him, shouting and wailing. Hastily, the seamen formed a circle around the bosun. Then, like an enormous crab, they backed away, making for the tenuous shelter of one of the huts.

Jack had heard the uproar and knew that his own moment had come. The two guards outside his hut were staring at the village, standing with their backs to him. He nodded at Mason and the two men moved forward together with their makeshift clubs. They struck at the same time. The guards collapsed at their feet.

'Come on!' Jack said.

The three of them slipped out into the shadows.

Down at the beach, two of De Witt's seamen were waiting with the jolly boat. They had heard the shots — there had been several more in the

66

last few minutes — and they were standing up to their knees in the water, anxious to be away. So they were relieved when they saw three shapes come sprinting out of the darkness and make for them.

'Here!' one of them hissed.

It was a mistake. Jack was the first to reach them. Mason and Pat were close behind. A second later, the jolly-boat was moving swiftly away from the shore leaving three unconscious men lying stretched out on the sand.

In the village, the battle raged on. The bosun and his men were trapped inside the hut — a hut that they would never leave. Still they fired, shot after shot tearing through the thin walls and ploughing into the Maoris who were grouped outside. But the warriors were relentless. As one fell another would move forward, hurling his spear towards the enemies.

The seamen had fire-power. The Maoris had strength of numbers. And in battle they were utterly without fear. Death meant nothing to them so long as they took their enemy with them. It was an uneven contest. Soon it was over.

From the *Sea Wolf*, Captain De Witt heard the last shots and the screams of the bosun as he was dragged out of the hut.

'Sounds like Campbell's got himself into trouble' he muttered to himself. He spat into the water. It was too bad that he wouldn't be able to use any of the Maoris for his gold prospecting. But he was safe. That was all that mattered. And he somehow expected that young Maru wouldn't be too popular with the tribe the next morning — that at least was something to smile about.

'Throw down your arms, Captain.'

De Witt turned round, his eyes widening in shock.

Jack Vincent stood there, Mason and Pat with him. De Witt glanced over his shoulder. What few men were left to him were grouped together at the far end of the deck. None of them were moving and De Witt could see why. Mason had taken over the ship's cannon. He had swivelled it round so that it now faced back into the ship. Back towards them. There was a burning taper in his right hand.

'Try anything and I'll blow holes through the lot of you,' Jack said.

De Witt forced the smile back to his lips. It wasn't easy. The smile sat there, wobbling slightly. 'Ah now, Mr Vincent,' he rasped. 'I thought you and I understood each other.'

'I think we do, Captain. Throw down your arms, all of you!'

A variety of weapons clanked and clattered on to the deck. The crew wasn't going to argue — not with a cannon.

De Witt licked his lips, trying to get them to work. 'Join me and you'll get your share of the gold,' he said. 'I give you my word.'

'I don't give a ship's biscuit for your word,' Jack replied. 'Over the side!'

De Witt stared at the coast, his eyes filled with terror. 'But they'll kill us!'

'That's your problem.'

One after another the seamen jumped. De Witt was the last to go. He turned to Jack with pleading eyes, but Jack shook his head. De Witt had planned to betray the Maoris. He would have enslaved them first, killed them later. It was only

68

just that he should go back and face them.

Jack waited until the bulky body of the captain had hit the water. Then he turned to Pat and Mason.

'Up anchor!' he commanded. 'Mason, set the main tops'l. Pat, you take the fore' course.'

They were fortunate. Had De Witt's ship been anything bigger than a caravel, they would never have been able to sail it. Even so, the next few minutes were a flurry of activity as they yanked on ropes and opened out the sails. And all the time they had to keep one eye open for the Maoris. They would be dealing with De Witt and the others to begin with. But sooner or later their thoughts would turn to the *Sea Wolf* itself . . .

At last the sails opened. The anchor cleared the surface of the water and the ship sailed smoothly out. But the night still brought one last surprise.

A single canoe had pursued them, slipping away from the beach. Mason saw it first and Jack had been ready with a musket to blow whoever was inside it into the next world. At the last moment, though, he stopped himself. There was only one person inside the canoe. It was Maru.

Maru had drunk nothing that night. As De Witt had correctly guessed, his stock had been low in the village. After all, the war with the Ngati Miru had been his idea, along with the need to buy muskets. He had also been angry about losing his pakehas. He had stolen away to watch over them. He had seen them escape. And he had followed them.

Now he stood in front of them on the boat.

'You people belong to me,' he said. 'Where I go, you go too.'

'Belong to you?' Vincent was too tired to

69

argue. 'Nice to have you aboard, sir,' he said mockingly.

Picking up speed, the *Sea Wolf* slid into the night.

5

As soon as it was light enough to see, Jack put the *Sea Wolf* through her paces. With the wind full behind her and the sails billowing, the ship surged forward, leaping over the waves, and her new master laughed with the sheer joy of it.

'She's a beauty, Jack!' Pat exclaimed, standing beside him at the wheel.

'Take her!'

Pat hesitated, then took the wheel. At once he felt the ship respond as he turned her first one way then another. It was like nothing he had ever experienced before. He and the *Sea Wolf* were one. They had absolute power over the ocean that was their domain. Pat had once been a convict. Now he had discovered a freedom that he had never thought he would find.

The other two passengers were less happy.

As ever, Mason had found something to grumble about. This time it was the sleeping quarters. 'He takes the only decent berth while we all swing in the foc'sle,' he muttered, glaring at Jack. He looked round as Maru walked past, carrying a bundle of stones. 'And what the devil's our lord and master up to now?' he demanded.

Maru took out one of the stones and held it up.

'This is from "umu",' he announced. An umu was a sort of oven.

'Oh, really?'

'These stones will keep my boat safe.' Maru tied the bundle to the ship's railing. 'They will keep you, my warriors, safe. Ka whakanoa koutou!'

'And the same to you,' Mason said and strode off down to the galley to find something to eat.

His mind was on other things: Pat, smiling like an idiot as he steered the *Sea Wolf*, and Mr High-and-Mighty Vincent acting like some sort of antipodean admiral. Muttering to himself, Mason opened the galley door and found himself face to face with a grinning Chinaman. Mason blinked. The Chinaman nodded politely. Mason whipped out a knife. The Chinaman leapt back, his hands up and his legs bent like some sort of ballet dancer. Mason stared. Neither of them spoke.

The Chinaman was short and stocky, in his mid-forties. But what on earth was he doing in the kitchen of a Portuguese ship stolen from a Dutch captain and now sailing in the middle of the South Seas? Mason did not bother to ask.

'Right, you slanty-eyed Chink . . .' he growled. 'On deck.'

Slowly, he advanced on the Chinaman. What happened next was so fast and so unexpected that Mason missed most of it. All he knew was that one moment he'd been standing up holding a knife, and the next he was lying on the floor with a terrible pain in his elbow, and that the Chinaman was now walking out of the galley.

'Pat!' he yelled. 'Get yourself down here!'

Meanwhile, Jack was working in De Witt's

72

cabin, going through some of the ex-captain's papers. A small tea-chest stood on the table in front of him, its lid open. Out of it, Jack had taken a handful of gold coins, a map, a journal and a leather bag. He had been about to open the bag when he had heard the commotion from the galley. He had heard Pat run down through the hatch and then there had been a second crash, a brief Irish shriek and finally silence. Then the door of the cabin burst open. Jack's hand reached for his knife as the Chinaman approached. The Chinaman came right up to the table, looming over him.

'It is midday. Precisely.' His English was perfect, with just the hint of a Scottish accent. He leant down and placed a tray on the table. It was piled high with food. 'The captain always eats at noon,' the Chinaman went on. 'It is an established tradition.'

A few moments later, Mason and Pat arrived. Mason's arm hung limp down his side and he was clutching the elbow with his other hand. Pat's nose was bleeding and his eyes were watering furiously. Maru appeared behind them, obviously baffled. Jack looked up at the little group clustered in the doorway and raised a glass of wine.

'Looks like we've inherited a cook,' he smiled.

His name was Su Shen Li, but everyone just called him Li. His story was a strange one even by South Sea standards where myth and legend seemed to be intertwined with day to day events.

His father was a warlord of the Emperor's Imperial Guard in China. In a society where status was the most important thing in a man's

73

life, Li had dared to fall in love with a girl outside his class, a commoner whose name was Meizhu. The two of them had run away together but inevitably they had been tracked down by the warlord's soldiers. Li had been forced to watch as the Imperial Executioner dismembered first Meizhu and then every member of her family. He himself had then been stripped of rank and banished for as long as his father lived.

He had taken passage on a French merchantman, but the captain, a vicious drunk by the name of Paul Chevalier, had robbed him and abandoned him in the Solomon Islands. That was where he had met De Witt who was trading for pearls. De Witt had needed a chef. Li had needed a job to survive. And so the warlord's son had ended up as a ship's cook.

Fortunately, Li's talents extended beyond the galley. He had already demonstrated his knowledge of the martial arts and he also knew his way around a ship. So, with Maru, Pat and Mason, he became the fourth member of the crew and the burden of work became a little lighter all round.

In the days that followed, the *Sea Wolf* made steady progress. The wind held and the weather was fine. Anyone coming on board would have considered them a motley crew — two Englishmen, an Irishman, a Chinaman and a Maori, but between them they had managed to restore the ship to something of her former glory and they were beginning to live with each other's habits and to learn each other's skills.

Maru, who had never been aboard such a ship before, soon became an accomplished sailor, climbing the rigging as if he'd been born to it and even taking over at the wheel. Li taught him how

74

to use the quadrant and the two of them often spent hours together, fishing. Pat took up caulking. Mason leant a hand patching the sails. And if there were times when they were edgy or uncooperative, at least they were no longer at each other's throats.

But the one thing nobody knew was — where were they heading?

Jack spent much of the time alone in De Witt's study, poring over the maps and the journal that he had found in the tea-chest. Occasionally he would give Mason a new bearing and Mason would grudgingly oblige, spinning the wheel five degrees windward or whatever. From his position at the wheel, Mason could see into the captain's cabin. He had to squat and peer through the companionway, but it was enough to allow him to spy on Jack. And now his curiosity was aroused. Jack hadn't discussed the journals he had found. Mason wouldn't have been able to read them if they'd been given to him . . . and nor, for that matter, could he have worked out the course that Jack was plotting on the charts. But once he had caught sight of a glimmer of gold, one of the coins. And often he had seen Jack thoughtfully weighing a small leather bag in his hand as he worked.

Mason was determined to find out what was inside the leather bag and one morning his chance came.

They had been taking it in turns to stand watch, and that morning it was the Irishman's turn. But Pat, who was never at his best in the morning, had rolled over in his bunk and gone back to sleep, leaving the ship unguarded. Mason tiptoed out. The captain's cabin was locked, but as ever the lock meant nothing to him.

In the grey half-light of the early morning, he searched through the cabin, opening the lockers, being careful not to displace anything he found. Everything was silent except for the creaking of wood and the rustle of cloth as the *Sea Wolf* rocked at anchor. At last he came upon the tea-chest and carried it over to the table. The chest wouldn't open to his prying fingers. Mason took out his knife and sprang the lock.

The charts and the journal he set aside. They meant nothing to him. But at the bottom of the tea-chest he found what he had been looking for: the leather bag. As he held it in the palm of his hand, something rattled inside. He forced his finger into the loop that tied the bag, loosened it, then held it upside-down. Eleven round, milky-white objects rolled out, each one about the size of a pea.

Mason stared at them for a long time. He was aware of a pain in his chest and suddenly realized that he was no longer breathing. With a slow smile, he forced himself to relax. So this was Master Vincent's treasure! No wonder he hadn't mentioned it to any of the others, for it was a treasure indeed.

Mason was holding eleven pearls. They were flawless and larger than any pearls he had ever seen. He looked at them thoughtfully. He would have to play his hand carefully. Nobody must know what he had discovered. But if things went the way he wanted them to, Jack Vincent, the *Sea Wolf*, the pearls . . . everything would be his.

Two days later, Mason made his move.

Jack had been behind the wheel for the entire

morning and was relieved by Maru, who had learnt so much about navigation in the past few days that he could now be trusted to command the *Sea Wolf* on his own. As was his custom, Jack went down to the cabin for an hour's rest before doing whatever work had to be done on deck. He opened the door and moved in. There was a movement behind him. He just had time to see a hand holding a belaying pin. The hand arched down towards him. He heard the sound of the heavy wooden club crashing into the back of his head and wondered vaguely if his skull had been broken. Then he was out.

When he came to, his hands and legs were tied. He had been positioned so that he faced the table and now Mason was sitting there, swinging the bag of pearls in front of him. Mason . . . that was hardly a surprise. Jack groaned, and not just because of the pain in his head. He was angry with himself. This was just the sort of thing he should have expected.

'Pearls,' Mason said. 'Where did they come from?'

'Oysters,' Jack replied.

Mason smiled mirthlessly. Getting up, he walked round the table, then lashed out with his foot, catching Jack in the ribs. 'Where did they come from?' he asked again.

'Read De Witt's journal, Mason,' Jack replied through gritted teeth. He cradled his ribs with the side of his arm. 'You can't, can you?' he went on. 'Can't read. Can't write. Can't navigate.'

Somebody stepped forward behind him and Jack looked round. It was Pat. Mason had told the Irishman everything, and although he looked distinctly unhappy about it, he had been waiting

in the cabin with him and had helped tie Jack up.
'Jack . . . please,' he entreated.

Jack sighed. 'All right,' he said. 'We're heading
for the island that was De Witt's base. He'd been
working these waters for years — slaving, thieving . . . anything that would show a profit. All he
made or stole, he traded for pearls.'

'Why?' Pat asked.

'Easy to transport. Easy to hide. Just the
thing to take back to Europe.'

'So why didn't you tell us?'

It was Pat who asked the question and Mason
who provided the answer. 'There is no island,' he
sneered. 'And there are no other pearls. There's
enough here for one of us — and that one was
going to be him. The first land we came to he'd
have been off and away and we'd have never
known nothing about no pearls.'

'You're out of your mind, Mason,' Jack said.
'There's more wealth on that island than you've
ever dreamed of. If you could read, you'd see it
for yourself. All we have to do when we get there
is row ashore and pick it up.'

'Captain Vincent has spoken the truth!'

The words came from the doorway. Li was
standing there, holding a knife. Now he stepped
into the room and before anyone could protest, he
leant down and cut Jack free. Then he moved
leisurely forward and picked up one of the charts.
Neither Pat nor Mason tried to stop him. They
had both had a taste of his strange fighting
abilities and once was very definitely enough.

'This is De Witt's camp,' Li said, pointing. 'On
the north shore.'

'Guarded, I suppose,' Mason muttered.

Li shook his head. 'I give you my word. Cap-

78

tain De Witt left no one. He didn't trust his crew.'

Rubbing his ribs where Mason had kicked him, Jack tapped the map with his forefinger. 'I thought we'd run ashore here,' he said.

'March overland?' Pat asked. 'Approach from the blind side?'

'Yes. That is — if Mason agrees.'

Mason nodded, scowling. 'You could have told us in the first place,' he said.

'He doesn't trust us.' Pat's voice was full of sadness. 'Just like De Witt. Isn't that it, Captain? You don't trust any of us.'

It took them another forty-eight hours to arrive at De Witt's island, two days in which there were no further incidents. Li had seen to that. The Chinaman managed to keep himself in sight of everyone just about all the time and under his watchful eye Mason would never have tried anything. There was something strange about the way Li regarded his crew members now that the pearls had been discovered. It was as if he knew something that they didn't.

They anchored the *Sea Wolf* in four fathoms of water, just off the coast. Jack and Mason were the first ashore, sailing together in the jolly boat. A wooded hillside led up almost from the water's edge. Jack was holding De Witt's map and after studying it, he gestured at Mason. The old sailor took a deep breath. The hill was steep, the path rough and uneven. But with a fortune of pearls waiting for him, Mason would have climbed an erupting volcano if he'd had to.

Even so, the journey upwards, with a hot sun overhead, just about finished him. It was one of the few times that he wasn't complaining, for he didn't have breath to utter the words. When he reached the top he dropped to the ground, grunting and blowing, then emptied a whole water bottle. Meanwhile, Jack had taken a telescope from his pocket and was scanning the coastline below. So far so good. There was nobody in sight.

Their path took them on through a forest with brightly-coloured flowers peeping out of the tropical grass and thick creepers hanging down like the rigging of a capsized ship. There was a thick, heavy silence in the forest — a silence that was suddenly broken by the muttering of voices and the crash of heavy feet marching through the undergrowth.

'Quick!' Jack threw himself behind a bush, dragging Mason with him. A moment later, three men appeared, sailors dressed in the faded uniforms of the British navy. Carrying baskets of wild berries and pine kernels, they walked past, talking among themselves.

'So much for Li's word,' Mason whispered.

'Let's follow them,' Jack said.

The two of them got up and, keeping a safe distance between them and the others, continued through the forest. The trees ended abruptly and the ground sloped away, running down to an extraordinary complex standing out in the open.

At first sight it looked like a military camp. There was a wooden stockade running all the way round the compound, the wood brand new in places where it had been repaired. Half a dozen huts stood inside with an animal pen directly behind them. Outside the stockade, three crosses stood in a forlorn group in a tiny cemetery. But before Mason or Jack saw any of this, their eyes were drawn to the parade ground at the heart of the compound. In the centre of the parade ground there was a flagpole. And from the flagpole fluttered a Union Jack.

'What the . . .?' Mason began.

The three men that they had followed had reached the compound and the gates were opened to allow them in. Jack took the telescope out again and squinted through it. Somebody had walked out of one of the huts and was crossing the parade ground. He adjusted the focus of the telescope. His body stiffened.

He had found De Witt's hide-out. If he could get in there, he would lay his hands on a fortune in pearls.

But Lieutenant Harry Anderson, former master of the *Success* had found it too. Anderson was alive. He had made it to the island. The feud was about to begin all over again.

6

'Right island. Right camp. Wrong time . . .'

Jack sat staring gloomily at a table piled high with food. He was back on the *Sea Wolf* and had told Pat, Maru and Li what he and Mason had found. The Chinaman had seemed less perturbed by the news than the others and had set about preparing an evening meal of fresh fish and fruit. But nobody was eating it. They could hardly believe what had happened. They had found the island. They knew where to find the pearls. But thanks to the unlucky reappearance of Anderson, they were stuck. It wasn't just their appetite they'd lost. It looked like they'd lost a fortune too.

'Maybe they've already found the pearls,' Pat said.

Jack threw down his knife. 'Don't be a fool. They couldn't know they're there. Our only problem is getting them out.'

'They outnumber us four to one,' Mason said. 'And Anderson's running the place like a land-locked man-o'-war.' He turned to Jack. 'I reckon we should up anchor and get out of here while we can.'

'No!' Maru had been concentrating hard, making sure he understood every word of what was being said. Now he spoke, and the ferocity in his voice surprised them all. 'Never give up fight without sending scout. Maru moves softly like a dragonfly. I will go. They will get a big surprise.'

Mason laughed scornfully and poured himself a glass of rum. But Jack was looking at the Maori thoughtfully. A plan had come to him. Maru was black. If he was washed up on the shore, found unconscious near the stockade, what would Anderson and his men do? They wouldn't think of him as a threat. They'd probably take him in, wait for him to recover, try to find out where he'd come from. And with one man on the inside . . .

'Maru . . .' Jack began.

The jolly-boat. The *Success* dwindling into the distance. The waves chopping. Swaying. Silence.

'I'll find you! If I have to search every island in the Pacific!'

Harry Anderson twisted in his narrow bunk inside the stockade. He was having a nightmare. Every night he dreamt it. It still seemed incredible that he had survived it.

'I'd save your breath to whistle up the wind!'

The smiling, triumphant face of Jack Vincent appeared, hovering over the empty sea, then broke up like a cloud of smoke. Yes, the wind had come. For the first day it had blown strong and fresh and the tiny boat had made good progress.

'Two ounces of ship's biscuit and a quarter pint of water. That's all we're having, Mr Towers.'

'It's not enough, Mr Anderson.'

'I know that, Mr Towers . . .'

He had been determined. He would drink salt water if he had to, eat the very leather of his boots. But their meagre supply of food would last

83

them. He would survive to find Jack Vincent again. One day he would even the score.

He had survived the storm that had seen the destruction of the *Success*. He had survived thirst and hunger. He had survived the shroud of despair that had wrapped itself over his crew, tugging them towards their graves. Hatred had burned in him. And the heat of it had warmed them all.

Now Harry Anderson stretched himself out beneath the rough blankets that covered him. The next part of the dream was easier. He relaxed, his legs straight, his arms at his sides. Someone had once joked that Anderson slept at attention. It was a thought that pleased him. He was an officer in the navy. And whatever he was doing, whatever happened, he always would be.

And that was how he ran the stockade.

They had been delivered. The jolly-boat had been washed ashore on an island. It was a miracle. Not a single member of the crew had died (although three of them had only survived a few weeks after landing, carried off by weakness and disease). And on the island he had found the rough beginnings of a military compound. Anderson had set to work. With Mr Flack at his side and the other officers of the *Success* to support him, he had turned the stockade into the land-locked man-o'-war that Mason had described.

The Union Jack flew from dawn to dusk, ceremonially raised and lowered at the start and the end of the day. Everyone in the stockade lived in the strictest discipline. Twenty lashes for brawling. Fifty for stealing. There was even a makeshift gallows for any more serious offences.

'A tight ship, Mr Towers. Show weakness, there'll be chaos. Then none of us will survive this God-forsaken place.'

That had been his philosophy and it had worked. The running of the stockade had become a smooth operation. The sort of thing that would make the navy proud. Take the young savage they had come across that evening ... unconscious at the water's edge. He had only been found because Anderson insisted on a patrol of the compound every four hours. And his caution had paid off in more ways than one.

They had discovered some gold coins on the youth, probably stolen from a trader. If there was a trader nearby, that might mean salvation for all of them. And as a final bonus he could hang the youth the next morning. Well, he was a thief and it would be a good lesson for the men.

A smooth operation.

Anderson smiled in his sleep. If he had known that Jack Vincent was less than a hundred yards away and getting closer by the second, he might have slept less easily.

Jack pressed forward, his feet making no sound on the sand outside the stockade. It was a moonless night, perfect for what he had in mind. Pat was with him, but as he turned to whisper a command, he saw that the Irishman had stopped a few paces behind. He was crouching beside a tree, clutching his stomach.

Jack sighed. He had known from the day they had met that Pat wasn't exactly someone to trust in a fight. The trouble was, the young boy had too vivid an imagination. He could imagine his wounds before he got them and that made him too afraid to risk getting them. At least, that was Pat's explanation. But sometimes Jack wondered if the real explanation wasn't a lot simpler. Was Pat a coward?

Hastily, he doubled back and stood beside him. Pat looked up, his eyes filled with pain. 'It's my guts, Jack . . .' he groaned. Jack shook his head. 'Honest!' Pat pleaded. 'I've got these terrible gripes . . .'

'One more word and I'll leave you here alone.' Jack had had enough of the Irishman's malingering. He moved away, drawing ever closer to the wooden wall. He wasn't surprised to hear Pat pick himself up and follow.

The door to the stockade was barred, but even as Jack and Pat approached it slowly opened from within. The timing was perfect. Maru stood in the darkness, grinning with excitement. As Jack had guessed, none of Anderson's men had thought twice about a seemingly unconscious native washed up on their island. He had been put in a cell, but the door hadn't even been locked. And as soon as night had fallen he had crept out to wait for Jack and to breach the compound's defences in the simplest possible way.

'Anderson?' Vincent whispered.

'Sleeping,' Maru replied.

'Where?'

'Last hut.'

For a moment, Jack was tempted to search out his old enemy, but just then there was an agonized grunt from Pat who was now leaning over like a very old man, both arms wrapped around his stomach. 'For the love of Mike!' he hissed. 'Let's get the pearls and go . . .'

Together the three of them hurried through the

stockade in the direction of the animal pens. They had got about half way before the alarm was raised. How were they to have known that even here, on this deserted island, Anderson insisted on an all-night watch? One moment they were alone. Everything was dark and silent. There was nothing to stop them. The next they had frozen in their tracks as a bell rang out and fiery torches carried by half-awake men came dancing out of the huts, forming a circle around them.

Anderson was at their head. Gazing across the parade ground, through the crimson shadows that rippled across the ground, it was as if he had somehow crossed the frontier between reality and fantasy and drifted, fully conscious, into his nightmare. 'It's Vincent!' he yelled. 'Get after them!'

Jack grabbed hold of Pat and pulled him back towards the gate. 'This way . . .'

'Jack — I can't!'

And now Jack saw that Pat hadn't been malingering after all. The Irishman's face was damp with sweat, his eyes unfocused and staring. The torches were reflecting, bright red, against his cheeks. It looked as if he was burning up from inside.

'I want them alive!' Anderson's voice came from across the compound.

Looking about him, Jack made an instant decision. Roughly, he pushed Maru in the direction of the gate. 'Get back to the ship,' he said.

But Maru held his ground. 'You stay — I stay.'

'Just go!' Jack was in no mood for argument and hearing the urgency in his voice, Maru obeyed, sprinting away into the darkness. At

87

once Jack half-dragged the Irishman into the shelter of the nearest hut. Anderson's men were about twenty yards away, approaching slowly in case the two intruders were armed.

'Scatter your powder,' Jack ordered once they were inside. 'They must be short of shot by now and I'm damned if I'm going to supply my own firing squad.'

Pat did as he was told, but couldn't help muttering, 'He'll just hang us instead.'

Jack looked doubtfully at the Irishman. Pat was getting worse by the moment. Now his skin was puffy and swollen. His lips had gone an unpleasant shade of blue. 'I wouldn't worry,' he said. 'He probably won't get a chance. And I thought you were malingering . . .'

'I wish I was.' Pat sighed. 'You should have gone with Maru while you had the chance.'

Outside, Anderson's men had surrounded the hut. For what seemed like a long time, nothing happened. The sailors were too afraid to go in. Then Anderson shouted an order in a quivering, almost hysterical voice. 'Get them!'

Jack shook his head. There was no point in prolonging it. He put down his gun and walked out into the glare of the torchlight. He was surrounded by a circle of unfriendly faces. This was the man who had stolen their ship. This was the man who had set them adrift with just eighty pounds of biscuits and a few barrels of water. But for this man, they would have all been on their way home, back to their wives and families.

Jack Vincent smiled and bowed. 'Good evening,' he said.

* * *

At dawn the next morning, Jack stood in front of Anderson in his hut. It seemed that they had come full circle. Once before he had stood in this position — on the *Success*. He had managed to reverse the position then, but this time it didn't look as if he was going to be so lucky. His hands were tied. Pat sat hunched up on the floor, groaning.

'Where's the *Success*?' Anderson asked.

'She went down,' Jack said.

Vincent examined him carefully. 'You're lying.'

'Couple of days after we put you over the side. A storm drove her on to a reef. Tore the bottom clean out.'

'Any survivors?'

Jack shrugged. 'You're looking at them. We got away on a grating and twelve feet of mizzen. The Maori and his people found us. We came here in his outrigger . . . as far as the reef anyhow.'

'Why in hell's name did you come here?' Anderson demanded. 'It can't have been family feeling.'

This was the question Jack had been dreading. The last thing he wanted to do was to let Anderson know about the pearls. There was a long silence. Then he was saved by Pat who suddenly began to retch, his body twitching and writhing on the floor.

A grey-haired man, whom Jack recognized as the ship's surgeon, bustled forward and knelt down beside Pat. 'What's wrong with him?' Jack asked.

Towers reached for Pat's pulse. 'Has he eaten anything here on the island?'

Jack thought back. 'He picked some fruit — large red berries.'

'Where did he find them?'

'A horseshoe bay on the south side.'

Towers sighed and dropped Pat's wrist. 'He's been poisoned,' he said.

'Well, for pity's sake do something!' Jack pleaded.

Anderson got up, a thin smile on his face. 'It's up to you, Jack,' he said. 'Tell me why you came and Towers will do everything he can. Otherwise you can watch him die and I'll see you dance on the gallows this very morning.'

Jack looked from Pat to Anderson. The surgeon was kneeling, staring at the lieutenant in disbelief, but Jack had no doubt that Anderson would live up to his word. He could watch a man die and think no more about it than if he had just trodden on an ant.

He had no choice. 'Pearls,' he said.

The single word hung in the air. 'A king's ransom, Harry,' Jack went on. 'They were hidden on the island by the previous tenant.'

Anderson shook his head slowly. 'You can do better than that.'

'His name was De Witt, a trader of sorts. His ship was wrecked near to where the Maori found us. I swam out to it. His journal was still in his cabin. I read it. Why else do you think I came ashore?'

'Where?'

For the first time since his capture, Jack felt a little more relaxed. There could be no mistaking the gleam of avarice in Anderson's eye. Now he had something to bargain with. 'If I tell you where they are, what's to prevent you hanging us both?' he asked.

'My word,' Anderson said.

Jack didn't even try to stop himself smiling. 'If the boy survives, you get the pearls,' he countered. 'Sooner or later a trader or a whaler will put in here for water. 'We stay alive until then — on your honour.'

'Anderson looked away. 'Very well . . .'

'Say it!'

He swung round and his eyes were cold. 'I swear you'll live to stand trial! Though heaven knows it will only delay the inevitable.'

Anderson didn't kill Jack. But in the days that followed he did everything in his power to make his enemy look forward to death.

Jack was tied to the mast beneath the Union Jack. He was given only enough water to keep him alive, never enough to slake his thirst. As an added cruelty, his food was heavily salted. The more he ate, the thirstier he became. Sitting in the open, without any shelter, he had no protection from the sun. Soon his skin blistered and cracked. It was as if he were being flayed alive. Every movement caused him torment and even the wind stroking his neck was enough to make him cry out in pain.

At the same time, Pat was allowed to be treated by the surgeon. Towers had seen the effects of the poisoning. Two of the sailors had eaten the same berries and would have died had it not been for him. The cure was simple. Pat was forced to drink water. If he was sick, he would be made to drink again. In this way his stomach was thoroughly cleaned out before too much of the poison could seep into his bloodstream. After five days he was able to eat. By then Jack was barely able to breathe.

But once again Anderson had miscalculated. His men had no reason to love Jack Vincent, but they could not witness their lieutenant's sadism without some feeling of revulsion. They understood nothing of the feud. Even if they had, they wouldn't have cared. There was something about Anderson that wasn't quite human. Either that or he was going insane.

Nobody was allowed to go near Jack, but after a week, and with Pat now well on the way to full recovery, Towers disobeyed. The surgeon was a strange man. Aware of his duty as an officer in the Royal Navy on the one hand — he would have followed Anderson to the ends of the earth rather than betray him — he could not forget his calling as a surgeon on the other. He was meant to be a healer, and yet all too often it was Anderson who had caused the wounds in the first place. Seeing Jack's prolonged torture beneath the flag, his conscience was torn two ways. But at last he acted. The officer deserted his post. The surgeon gave Jack water.

'I'm obliged,' Jack gasped as the water trickled over his chin and on to his chest, 'Pat . . .?'

'Weak, but on the mend.' Towers looked around anxiously. There was nobody in sight but at any moment the midday guard would be parading in the square. 'Vincent,' he said. 'The minute you find the pearls, Anderson means to convene a court martial. He'll try and condemn you himself, fairly and according to Naval regulations.'

'Unless you set me free and turn your back,' Jack muttered.

Towers straightened up, the water-cup falling from his hand. 'Ignoring the fact that you are an escaped convict with several capital offences outstanding, what you are asking would amount to mutiny!' he exclaimed.

But Jack had got the measure of his man. He pressed on. 'Harry Anderson is insane,' he said. 'Any court martial carried out by him would be a travesty of justice.' Towers opened his mouth to argue, but there was nothing he could say. Jack pressed on, his words soft and determined. 'I have a ship at a safe anchorage down the coast. I'll take you with us. If you pick up a merchant-man in Tahiti you could be back in England by Christmas.'

The old surgeon's mouth fell open. Suddenly his eyes were far away.

'Don't you have a family, man? Friends . . . the people you've left behind? You owe it to them!'

'If . . .' Towers paused on the word. 'If I agreed, how would you reach your ship? Anderson has a guard on the gate.'

Jack smiled. 'Don't worry about the guard,' he said. 'I have a plan . . .'

That night, Towers slipped out of the stockade.

Only Jack saw him go. Anderson and the others were roasting a wild pig over a fire, an open-air barbecue made strangely grotesque by the single man tied to the mast. Jack had been invited to the feast. But, of course, he had been given nothing to eat. The whole thing was only being staged to torture him further. In a way, Jack was grateful for it. If Towers had had any doubts about the right course of action, this new display decided him. Anderson was standing beside the pig, cutting himself some pork. But his eyes had never left his prisoner. Jack was careful not to give anything away by smiling.

Even so, he couldn't relax. He knew that Towers still owed his first loyalty to Anderson and

93

might at any time go back on their arrangement. It was only on the afternoon of the following day that he realized his plan was working. That was when Towers announced that he and Mr Flack had found Jack Vincent's ship.

There was an immediate commotion in the stockade. The *Sea Wolf* was as important to Anderson as it had been to Jack when he had been a prisoner on the Maori's island. According to Towers, there had only been one man on look-out, and he and the bosun had been careful not to be seen themselves. So that meant that Anderson and the others could take the ship by surprise! A short struggle and it would be theirs.

Scarcely able to control his glee, Anderson marched out of the stockade leaving only one man on guard behind him. It was exactly what Jack had hoped he would do. As soon as they were alone, Jack called out to him.

'Guard! I'm thirsty . . .!'

'Go to the devil!'

'I'll pay for it.'

As the guard approached, Vincent reached down to his boot. From there he produced a gold coin. The guard smiled and bent down to take it. He didn't hear Towers creep up behind him. He didn't see the broken wooden club that the surgeon was holding. In truth, he didn't even feel the blow that struck him on the back of the neck. It was medically precise. The guard was out like a light.

Towers looked at the fallen figure, his face filled with regret, then he collected himself and cut Jack free. A minute later the two had unlocked the door of Pat's cell and Jack was delighted to see the Irishman leaping to his feet, his face full of colour — the right colour — and the fever gone.

'Come on!' Jack said. 'The pigpen . . .'

'But . . .' Pat began.

Ignoring him, Jack ran across to the other side of the compound where Li was already waiting for him. It was Li that Towers had met the night before, guarding the ship as Jack had said he would be. The surgeon had almost fallen victim to one of the Chinaman's rabbit punches, but had just been able to identify himself in time.

All the same he kept his distance now as Jack climbed into the pigpen and thrust his hand deep into the mud in the far corner. For perhaps thirty seconds he remained there, elbow-deep in the filth. But when he drew it out he was clutching another leather sack, five times the size of the one he had found on the *Sea Wolf*.

'All right. Let's get out of here,' he said.

'I'm not coming with you.' Towers shook his head, leaning against the pigpen.

'Why not?' Jack demanded.

'I've thought long and hard about it,' the surgeon sighed. 'And I can't.' He drew a deep breath. 'I don't believe Anderson is insane, but another month on this God-forsaken rock, and he surely will be.'

'That's all the more reason . . .' Jack began.

'No. He's already pushed the crew to their limit. If I go, God knows what will happen.' Jack made to speak again, but Towers stopped him. 'It's my duty, Vincent.'

'Very well.' Jack balanced the pearls in his hand. The sack felt heavy. The heavier the better. He turned to go, but then turned round again. 'Then why?' he asked. 'Why have you helped me?'

95

'If Anderson's mad, you're part of that madness,' Towers replied. 'I think it's better — healthier — for all of us if you go. And for what it's worth, although, as my Commanding Officer he is entitled to absolute loyalty, on a personal level I can't abide the man.' Towers stuck out a hand. 'Safe journey, Jack Vincent.'

Jack took the hand. 'You're a true gentleman, Mr Towers.'

But there was still one piece of unfinished business. Towers handed Jack the piece of wood and turned his head. 'Just hard enough to be convincing,' he said.

Jack lifted the piece of wood and knocked out the man who had just saved his life.

Meanwhile, Anderson was feeling like knocking out Towers and the bosun too.

'She was here, Captain,' Mr Flack was saying. 'Right in-shore, Captain. I swear it!'

Anderson looked out with flat, empty eyes at a flat, empty sea. There was no sign of the *Sea Wolf*, no sign even of its jolly-boat.

'At least we've still got Vincent, sir,' the bosun added.

Anderson felt something cold in the pit of his stomach. Vincent . . .? But no, it was impossible. Vincent couldn't have set this up. He had been tied up, helpless. *And Anderson had just walked out of the stockade leaving only one man to guard him!*

'Back!' he yelled. 'Get back to the camp!'

He was already on his way, clambering up the hill that Jack and Mason had climbed on their first visit to the island. From there he ran on, crashing through the forest. It was when he

96

reached the edge that he saw his worst fears had been realized. Jack Vincent had escaped from him again.

The jolly-boat was cutting out from the headland, ploughing into the surf. The *Sea Wolf* was waiting for it, having sailed serenely round the island while he and his men marched across. He could see Jack sitting at the bow with the Irishman and what looked like a Chinaman. And he could see the leather bag that rested in Jack's hand.

With a howl of rage, he seized the musket from Mr Flack and loaded it, doubling the amount of gunpowder to give his shot extra range. The bosun looked on in dismay. 'It's an old gun, Mr Anderson,' he warned. 'A double charge will likely split the barrel . . .'

But Anderson didn't listen. Vincent was getting way. He had the pearls. Anderson had been tricked once again. But this time he wouldn't escape unscathed. Anderson brought the musket up and aimed. There he was. Vincent was in his sights. He pulled the trigger.

The gun exploded. Fragments of metal tore into Anderson's face. He was thrown off his feet unable to hear anything except the ringing in his ears. There was a dull pounding in his head and for a moment he wondered if he had managed to blind himself. But then his vision cleared — and there was Vincent, still sailing away but now he was kneeling over the Irishman, holding him where he had been wounded in the neck.

Anderson scrambled to his feet and stood there swaying, the blood running down his cheeks like tears. 'It isn't over yet, Vincent!' he screamed. The words echoed across the waves. 'I'll chase you to the gates of hell if I have to!'

The jolly-boat pulled alongside the *Sea Wolf* where Mason and Maru were waiting to greet it. Anderson wiped blood from his face. Then, with a final curse, he spun on his heels and marched back to the stockade.

7

Pat was lucky. An inch to the left and Anderson's bullet would have torn out his windpipe. As it was, it had passed through the skin on the side of his neck, leaving a scar that would be with him until the end of his days, but no major damage. And by the time the *Sea Wolf* had left De Witt's (or Anderson's) island far behind it, he had completely forgotten the pain. There were more important things to occupy his mind.

'The pearls, Jack . . .' he said.

He and Jack were in the captain's cabin with Mason. The leather sack that he had retrieved from the pigpen now lay on the table, its contents scattered across the wooden surface. There were fifty-eight pearls; with the eleven they had already found that made sixty-nine altogether. How much would they be worth? Out here, of course, the answer was very little. But if they could ever get them back to Europe, — they would all be rich men.

'Time for the share-out,' Mason said, his eyes fixed on the table.

'A five-way split,' Pat added. 'Like we agreed.'

Jack smiled. 'The agreement stands. But for now they stay under lock and key.'

'The devil they do!' Mason exclaimed. His

hand reached out to scoop up the pearls but Jack stopped him.

'We'd be at each other's throats within a week,' he explained. 'No one would sleep for fear of being robbed, or worse.'

'It's a mistrustful mind you have, Jack Vincent,' Pat muttered. 'But I suppose it makes some sense.'

'How long?' Mason demanded.

'Just be patient, Mason,' Jack said. 'Provided nothing else happens to us, we'll all be able to go home and retire.'

But the very next day something did happen to them. It was the last thing they could have expected.

It was another bright, clear day. Jack had plotted a course that would, he said, bring them to the Solomon Islands where they would be able to sell the *Sea Wolf* and buy tickets on a larger ship heading for Europe. Maru was at the wheel, and it was he who saw it first.

'Jack!' he called out.

Jack appeared, climbing up through the hatchway, and gazed in the direction that Maru was pointing.

It was a skiff, bobbing up and down on the waves, a tiny boat with two figures in it, one lying down, one standing and waving. Jack looked about, expecting to see the ship from which it had come. But there was nothing. The skiff disappeared into a trough, then rose up again.

'Pat . . . Mason!' Jack called.

Taking over the wheel, he turned it hard to starboard, making for the skiff. With the strong wind and the high waves it was a difficult manoeuvre, but Jack had navy blood flowing in his veins. Soon he had brought the *Sea Wolf* abreast of the skiff and he was able to look down and see just who it was that he was rescuing.

It was a girl. If Jack was surprised, it was nothing to what Maru felt. He had never seen a white woman before and his eyes and his smile widened simultaneously. Even Mason uttered a low whistle. It wasn't that she was particularly beautiful (although after months at sea without a woman in sight any female company would have been welcome). But there was something about her, a wild, gypsy quality that set the pulse racing. Her hair was dark, her eyes deep and secretive. Although her skin had suffered from too much exposure to the sun, she had not suffered from lack of food or water. Whatever had happened to the ship she had come from, had obviously happened recently.

The other passenger in the boat was less well off. He was a naval officer — that you could tell from the torn and discoloured remains of his uniform. His face was pale, his eyelids puffy and swollen. Blood, trickling from an ugly head-wound, had reddened the water in the bottom of the boat. He was in his mid-thirties, Jack guessed — cold, authoritarian ... a typical career man.

'Gentlemen,' said Jack, as the *Sea Wolf* rubbed shoulders with the skiff, 'help the young lady aboard. And gently.'

'The good Lord save us!' Pat whispered, seeing the other man for the first time. 'A naval officer.'

'Maru!' The Maori snapped out of his trance as Jack called his name and helped the woman climb on to the boat. At the same time, Li and Mason pulled out the officer. 'Take him down below,'

Jack ordered. 'I'll look after the lady.'

'Typical,' Mason grunted, struggling under the weight. 'He gets the beauty. We end up lumping the beast!'

Her name was Sovay Banks. She had been in the skiff for six days, ever since a storm had sunk her ship. She and the lieutenant — his name was Piercey Grindall — had been the only ones to survive.

'How did he get his wound?' Jack asked. There was something strange about that wound. The lieutenant had been on board the skiff for six days but the wound could only have been a few hours old.

'We saw your sail,' Sovay explained. 'He fell trying to attract your attention.'

It was a convincing story, so why wasn't Jack convinced? 'What was your ship?' he asked.

'The *Falcon.* We were sailing for Norfolk Island ...' Jack's eyes narrowed. '... carrying troops to relieve the garrison. The Governor himself arranged passage for me. I was to marry his personal aide.' Her lip trembled and a single tear ran down her cheek. It was a pretty performance. But was it just a performance?

'The wound,' Li muttered, after Sovay had gone down to her cabin to rest. 'It could never have been caused by a fall. Something or someone hit him ...'

But there was nothing they could prove and for the time being Jack had decided to be hospitable to his new guests, Sovay in particular. As soon as she had woken up, he found her some new clothes which, being tailored for a man, showed off her figure in a way she might not have wished. But,

Jack was forced to admit, she certainly had a figure to show.

Then it was time for supper. Lieutenant Grindall had still not recovered consciousness, but Sovay ate enough for the two of them, watched by a strangely thoughtful Jack. He seemed to have lost his appetite too.

'Li will give you something for your sores when you've finished,' he said.

Sovay nodded her thanks, her mouth full.

'As you can see, we're not exactly rigged for female passengers. But you can take my cabin. Do you know your way about the ship?'

'Yes, thank you. Mr Mason showed me.'

Sovay finished her meal and got up. 'I'll say goodnight, then.'

Jack nodded and she moved away. But not in the direction of her cabin.

She waited outside in the gloomy corridor, making sure that nobody had followed her, then hurried along and down the first hatchway she came to. As soon as she had woken up she had asked Mason to take her to Lieutenant Grindall. Her eyes had been full of concern then. They were hard and coldly purposeful now.

She found the cabin again and went in, quietly closing the door behind her. The lieutenant lay in a deep sleep, but as she approached him he must have sensed her presence for his eyes flickered open. Without saying a word, she picked up a blanket and folded it. Now she was smiling, a thin, cruel smile of hatred. Before the sick man could cry out, she pressed the blanket down against his face and held it there with hands that had suddenly become claws. The lieutenant's body heaved and jerked but she was too strong for him. Slowly, he suffocated.

But then she was seized from behind, pulled away and sent spinning against the wall.

'Why?' Jack Vincent looked from her to Grindall.

'She's a convict.' The words, whispered painfully, came from the bed.

'Liar!' Sovay's eyes were night-black. She threw herself forward again, her nails reaching out and raking Jack's cheeks. For a moment it was as if she had gone berserk. Then, with an oath, he gained control and pushed her roughly back.

'My name is Grindall,' the sick man said. 'First Officer aboard His Majesty's prison hulk, *Owler.*'

'It's not true!' Sovay insisted.

'You were bound for the Norfolk Islands?' Jack asked.

Grindall nodded weakly. 'Take us there and I'll see you are rewarded.' His head fell back against the pillow.

'Li!' Vincent called.

Sovay moved towards him. She had managed to force the cruelty out of her face but Jack could still see it there, hidden behind the mask. 'Not another word!' Jack warned her.

'We floundered. Saw your ship . . . hell-hag . . . felled me with my own pistol.' Grindall's words trailed away as he drifted back into sleep.

Then Li appeared with Pat close behind him. The two men stared at Jack, waiting for an explanation. But explanations could wait.

'Lock her in the forward hold,' he said.

He rubbed a finger against his cheek. Sovay had drawn blood. He had known from the very start that she was a convict. Takes one to know one, he thought to himself and smiled wryly in the half-light of the cabin. But a murderess? Despite everything that had happened, despite what he had seen with his own eyes, he didn't believe it. Well . . . he would find out soon enough. And in the meantime he would keep a careful watch on both his uninvited guests.

The very next morning, Jack visited Sovay in her new cell in the hold. She was calmer now and answered his questions with a soft, expressionless voice.

'The convicts aboard the *Owler* were all women,' she explained. 'The gaolers and the crew were all men. Grindall singled me out. For three months he . . .' Tears of outrage welled up in her eyes and she was unable to go on.

'I can guess,' Jack muttered softly. 'But if you wanted to finish him, why didn't you put him over the side before we picked you up?'

'He was too heavy.' Sovay sighed. 'What will you do with me?'

'I don't know yet . . .' Jack straightened up and moved towards the door. 'But you can stake your life I won't be taking you to Norfolk Island.'

It was a bizarre situation. Sovay and Grindall had escaped from one convict ship, only to end up with the survivors of another. Obviously Jack couldn't take Grindall to Norfolk Island — it was the last place on Earth he'd have approached. And, as Mason had been the first to point out, there'd have been the devil to pay if the Lieutenant had found out who they were. They could of course overpower him and do Sovay's work for her, dumping him in the sea. But what-

105

ever else he was, Jack was no murderer. So he decided to keep things as they were. Sovay and Grindall would both remain on board, but out of each other's way. There would be no more murder attempts. And hopefully Jack would work out what to do.

Grindall recovered quickly enough and the next few days passed without any problems. Jack had told him they were heading for Norfolk Island and although the officer said nothing, he seemed surprised, staring at the stars by night and discreetly examining his compass by day. Only once did he raise the subject with Jack. It was early one morning, about a week after he had been strong enough to get out of bed. Mason was at the wheel. Maru was up in the halyards, unfurling the sails. Pat was swabbing. Sovay was sitting at the far end of the deck, alone.

'An eccentric course for Norfolk Island, sir,' he muttered.

'You've sailed the Pacific before?' Jack asked, equally casually.

'Yes. With Bligh.' He paused, allowing the last word to sink in. 'You know him, of course? Caught his mutineers. Took 'em home and hanged 'em.'

'Did he?' Jack sounded uninterested, but behind him Mason had frozen like a statue. 'Hold your course, Mason,' he said.

Grindall said no more. But from that moment something changed. He was as polite and formal as before, but he was also a little more distant, a little more wary. And two days later, he struck.

They had run low on water and had turned west to put in to land. It couldn't have happened at a worse time. Scanning the coastline, Maru

106

shook his head unhappily. 'This is not a good place for water, Jack,' he said. 'This is Ngapuhi territory.'

'Tribal enemies?' Jack asked.

'Ngapuhi are worthy of respect. They are warm and cold. They are . . . like all people. They have many faces.'

'You mean they're unpredictable?'

'Many faces.'

Pat had heard all this. 'So why don't we put in further down the coast?' he asked.

Maru shook his head again. 'They are worsely unpredictable.'

Once again, they didn't really have any choice. The jolly-boat was lowered and, taking a pile of barrels with them, Jack and Maru set off.

'Where's Grindall?' Jack asked Li before he pushed off.

'Resting,' the Chinaman said.

'Watch him . . .'

But it was already too late. Grindall wasn't resting. He had hardly rested from the time when he had drained the water butts to force the ship ashore. When Pat went down to swab the area where Sovay had been briefly imprisoned, Grindall was already there, waiting with a belaying pin in his hand. The Irishman was taken completely by surprise. One moment he was wringing the mop and whistling to himself, the next he was on his back, unconscious. A hand reached down and pulled the pistol out of his belt. When Grindall stepped out of the hold, he was armed.

Meanwhile, up on the foredeck, Li was gutting a fish, preparing lunch for Jack's return. Mason was standing a few feet away from him, watching

Jack and Maru through a telescope. The two of them had landed, possibly on hostile territory, but at least the beach looked empty. They were just lifting the first of the water butts on to the sand, talking to each other as they worked. Mason sniffed. He could smell something in the air. He sniffed again, then looked over his shoulder.

'Li! Pat!' he yelled.

Thick black smoke was seeping out of the cabin hatch, spreading over the deck and floating into the air. It was the worst possible thing that could have happened. The *Sea Wolf* was on fire.

The Chinaman dropped his knife and he and Mason leapt to the hatch, pulling it open. More smoke billowed out. Taking a deep breath, eyes streaming, they plunged into the opening and made their way down, determined to put the blaze out. It was only when they reached the bottom that they saw the cause of the fire — a burning mattress. Above them the hatchway slammed shut and they heard the lock being slid into place. They were trapped.

Jack was just rolling the first barrel off the beach when he heard an exclamation from Maru and saw the first wisps of smoke drifting across the sky. Maru was already running for the boat. With a curse, Jack leapt over the barrel and followed him.

On the *Sea Wolf* Grindall had reached the galley.

Pat was unconscious. Mason and Li were locked beneath the deck. That only left Sovay, and Grindall had a score to settle with her. He wouldn't kill her. Not yet. First they had some unfinished business . . .

108

He kicked the door open and strode into the galley, the gun in his hand, searching for her. He didn't see her, crouching behind the door, until it was too late. She was holding a skillet, a huge copper pan that Li had intended to use for the fish. Now she swung it with all her strength. It smashed into the side of Grindall's head, throwing him off balance. He stretched out a hand to steady himself, then shrieked with pain and anger as he made contact with the stove. The skin on his palm and fingers peeled away. Sobbing, he stuffed his hand into his mouth. If he had seen Sovay then he would have shot her. But already she had gone, diving through the starboard hold and into the shadows. Outside, Jack was shouting. The jolly-boat had arrived back at the *Sea Wolf*. Raising one foot, Grindall kicked the bolt across on the door of the hold. That would keep Sovay quiet until he came back for her. Then he went up on deck.

Maru was just climbing over the side of the ship when Grindall appeared. Jack called out a warning but Maru had no time to react. Grindall was holding another belaying pin. He threw it. It caught Maru right between the eyes, stunning him. Grunting, he twisted round and fell back on top of Jack. The two of them sprawled in the bottom of the boat. At the same time Grindall pulled the gun out of his belt and clumsily positioned it in his raw, blistering hand. The side of his face where he had been hit with the pan was horribly discoloured. One of his eyes was bloodshot. His hair was in disarray. Jack couldn't help thinking that right now Lieutenant Grindall looked more like an escaped lunatic than an officer in the Royal Navy.

109

Jack climbed on board the *Sea Wolf* and stopped dead as Grindall levelled the pistol at him. He glanced back at the jolly-boat. Maru was going to be no use to him. There was no sign of anybody else.

'Where are the others?' he asked.

'Later — Lieutenant Vincent.' Grindall spat out the last two words as if they'd left a sour taste in his mouth. Then he smiled. 'Yes,' he said. 'The name was vaguely familiar, right from the start. And when I saw the course you were plotting . . .'

'So what are you going to do?' Jack said. 'Hold us all at gunpoint until we get to Norfolk Island?'

'I don't care about you and your crew. All I want is passage — and the girl. Take us and you can sail away, I give you my word.'

'And if I refuse . . .?'

'Then I'll shoot you now.'

Grindall raised his gun. There was a sound behind him, a soft footfall on the deck. Sensing danger, the lieutenant spun round, just in time to see Sovay charge towards him. With a half-human snarl he aimed his gun at her. There was an explosion. The sound echoed across the water. On the island a flock of birds thundered out of the trees and scattered in the sky. Then there was a silence that seemed to last forever.

Grindall dropped his gun and fell to the deck. Jack was holding a gun, a second gun that he had carried with him from the moment the two castaways had come on board. A thin trickle of smoke curled upwards from the muzzle. Grindall pitched forward and lay still.

'Sovay . . .?' Jack said.

'I'm all right.' Sovay was beginning to shake.

110

'Where did you spring from?' Jack asked.

'He had me locked in the hold. But there's a loose plank. I got out and . . .' The words caught in her throat. Sovay looked at the dead man and wept.

They buried Grindall at sea. The ceremony would have been more moving if they hadn't been so glad to get rid of him. Sovay was still shaking after her ordeal. Pat was nursing a king-sized headache. Li and Mason were angry that they had been tricked so easily, and although they were untouched physically, their pride had taken a mauling. Maru would have an unpleasant black eye — not that you would be able to see it, as Mason had quickly pointed out. As for Jack, he would never have another comfortable night's sleep on board the *Sea Wolf.* The mattress that Grindall had burned had been his.

And the mattress hadn't been filled with just horse-hair.

It was Mason who had found it, once he'd put out the fire. It had been concealed behind a slit in the middle of the mattress and now he held it up for all to see. The leather bag containing the pearls. Mason grinned. 'Hidden in your mattress!' he exclaimed. 'I don't know how you ever managed to get a wink of sleep!'

The bag had been charred and blackened by the fire. A second later the smile was wiped off Mason's face as it disintegrated. Suddenly it was raining pearls. They bounced like glittering hailstones onto the deck.

'Damn your blood, Mason!' Jack swore. 'Pick them up!'

Pat was already on his knees. Mason joined him.

111

'I've counted every last one!' Jack warned them.

He watched as they collected the pearls. He watched as they refilled the tattered leather bag. He watched as they counted them and finally handed them back to him. But he didn't watch Sovay. That was a mistake because if he had, he would have seen that she was taking a real interest in the pearls.

And she wasn't shaking any more.

8

Everyone agreed that they needed a few hours' rest before they set sail again. Apart from anything else, Jack and Maru still hadn't filled the butts with fresh water, and while they went ashore with Pat (who claimed that his head still hurt too much for him to be able to do any work), Sovay, Mason and Li could get on with the job of cleaning up the *Sea Wolf*, clearing away the damage caused by the fire.

If Grindall had only waited a little longer before making his attempt to take over the *Sea Wolf*, he might have been more successful. That same afternoon they sighted a second ship, sailing slowly to the south, the American flag fluttering from its mast.

'A merchantman?' Mason asked.

'It's the *Kahore*,' Maru answered. 'Every year they come here to repair masts.' He pointed over the bay. 'Beyond the hills there is a harbour . . . of scrub with many kauri. It is these trees that the pakeha takes for his ships.'

Jack shrugged. 'Let 'em. As long as they're not interested in us.'

But one person on the *Sea Wolf* was very interested in the Americans. Sovay's eyes never left the whaler's sails until it had disappeared round the corner of the island. For the rest of the afternoon she was all smiles. Mason and Li had begun to think that she was one of them, and that they would all sail on together.

Unfortunately, Sovay had other ideas.

As soon as the whaler was out of sight, Jack set out again for land. He had not forgotten that this was the territory of the Ngapuhi and he made sure that everyone carried guns. Mason and Li had decided to come too in the end. It might be risky going on shore, but with perhaps a month or more at sea ahead of them, the temptation to set their feet on dry land was too great to resist.

They beached the jolly-boat at the foot of the crescent-shaped bay and crossed the sand to an inlet in the wood where they had already stacked the barrels. A fresh-water stream bubbled out of the wood here, and working as quickly as they could, they soon had the barrels loaded back in the boat and were about to leave when Pat gently touched Jack's arm.

'What ...?' Jack began. He turned round and stopped dead.

They were surrounded. Moving with the same almost magical stealth that Maru's own tribe had shown, they had crept out of the forest to circle the three men. Jack recognized at once the swirling patterns on their faces and the various weapons they carried: the whalebone spears or 'hoeroas', the black 'onewa' and the short clubs or 'patus'. Whatever their names, they all added up to the same thing — trouble.

Mason was already lifting his musket, but Jack stopped him. If they shot one of these Ngapuhi warriors, the rest of them would fall on them and cut them to pieces. Only Maru could save them now, and they stood silent and perfectly still as the young Maori ostentatiously took the knife and club out of his belt, laid them on the sand and stepped forward, unarmed, to talk to the Ngapuhi chief.

They talked for about five minutes. At one point, the chief gestured at the ship and said something which made Jack smile. Li looked at him curiously.

'You understand?' he asked.

'Some of it,' Jack muttered. In fact, after many hours spent in Maru's company he had managed to pick up a fair bit of Maori.

'What's that heathen scroat saying?' Mason demanded.

'He's recognized the ship,' Jack replied. 'He thinks De Witt has come to rob him.'

'God help us!' Pat whispered, his face going the colour of cheese.

Maru talked on, more animatedly now. He almost reminded Jack of a defence lawyer in a courtroom, arguing the case of the defendant. And what would be the verdict if they were found guilty? Somehow Jack didn't think the Ngapuhi would let them off with a warning!

But then Maru relaxed, bowed to the chief and walked back over to the group.

'Go,' he said. 'But not too quick.'

'I don't believe it . . .' Mason crowed.

'What did you say to him?' Pat asked.

They had pushed the jolly-boat off the sand and now they leapt into it, squatting beside the water barrels.

'What does it matter?' Maru asked. 'Your head still sits on your shoulders . . .'

* * *

Sovay almost fell into Jack's arms as he climbed back on to the *Sea Wolf*. 'I was sure they'd kill you,' she said.

'They would have if it hadn't been for Maru,' Jack told her.

'Thank you.' Sovay took Maru's hand and kissed it. The Maori was taken quite by surprise. Amongst his people, you rubbed noses to show affection. White women and kissing . . . it was all quite beyond him.

'We can sail on the night tide,' Pat said. As far as he was concerned, the sooner they were away from the Ngapuhi, the better.

But Jack shook his head. 'Not in these waters! We'll wait for morning.'

That evening they had a feast to celebrate their close escape. Jack broached another keg of De Witt's rum and Sovay prepared a special dinner. As ever, it was fish, but she also surprised Maru with a salad of sow-thistle and watercress, which were apparently Maori specialities. Maru was still glancing from time to time at the back of his hand as if he expected to find the imprint of her lips there, and it was obvious that he had completely fallen for their female passenger. Sovay was wearing a dress for the evening — she had made it herself from all the odds and ends she had been able to lay her hands on. With her hair combed back and a crystal glass in her hand, she looked every inch the lady.

'The lizard has changed into a kotuku,' Maru said.

'A kotuku?' Pat asked.

'A white heron!'

Sovay had cooked the meal herself and she also served it, making sure that everyone's plate was piled high. Then she went round, filling the glasses, or refilling them if they had already been emptied.

'The dinner is my way of thanking you, Jack Vincent,' she said.

Jack raised his glass to her. 'It's been a long time since I enjoyed such ... agreeable company.'

On the other side of the table, Mason nudged Li and gave him a great wink. He could tell what Jack was feeling for Sovay and to him it was a wonderful joke. Jack Vincent in love! Li, however, turned away. It was beneath his dignity to speculate on such matters.

'De Witt's pearls make you all wealthy men, do they not?' Sovay asked.

'I suppose so,' Jack said.

Sovay got up and went over to him, bending over his shoulder so that her lips brushed against his ear. 'A new life, Jack,' she whispered. 'Forget the others. Think of just the two of us together. Safe from the authorities.'

Jack smiled and shook his head. 'Sovay ...' he began.

'We could do anything. Be anything we want.'

'No ...'

Jack was suddenly angry ... and disappointed. What Sovay was suggesting was out of the question. He would never betray his friends, not for her, not for anything. He turned to speak to Mason and was surprised to see the old sailor slumped over the table. Surely he hadn't drunk as much as that? On the other side of the table, Li, tilted in his chair and sprawled out on the floor. Jack tried to stand up, but the strength seemed to have drained out of his legs. The whole room was racing away from him as if down a long tunnel. Maru was unconscious. So was Pat. He reached out for the table, trying to grab hold of it. But the table wasn't there any more. He was falling backwards. And there was Sovay, her face filling his vision, her eyes locked into his, regarding him with sadness . . . and perhaps with love?

It was the last thing he saw. The cabin reached the end of the tunnel, a tiny pin-prick of light that was suddenly extinguished. Jack toppled forward and lay still.

They all woke up at about the same time. It was the morning of the next day, the first rays of the sun slanting in through the window.

'My head . . .' Pat was holding it in both hands. 'What happened?'

Jack opened his eyes. There was a foul taste on his tongue. His mouth was dry. 'We were drugged,' he said. Unsteadily, he got to his feet and reached out for a bucket which he gave to Pat. 'You'll probably need this,' he said.

Ten minutes later, all five of them had assembled in Jack's cabin. Five of them. The sixth — Sovay — had gone.

'Mistress Banks . . .' Li muttered.

'Yes.' The bitterness of the drug lingered in Jack's voice.

'She used a sleeping draught,' Li said. 'Mixed with the liquor, it was very strong. I suppose she found it in the galley.'

'She'll be trying for the American whaler.'

'And good riddance to her,' Mason muttered.

Maru wasn't so sure. 'The kotuku is in danger,' he said in a low voice. 'The Ngapuhi will kill her.'

'That's her look-out,' Mason snarled.

'She's taken the pearls.'

Mason looked up, his mouth falling open. Jack was standing behind the table, holding an oilskin package. He let it fall on to the wooden surface. It was empty.

Mason snatched it up. 'I'll kill her!'

Jack ignored him. His face was tired, sad. Somehow, Li suspected, it wasn't the loss of the pearls that mattered to him. 'I'm going after her,' he said.

'I'll come too,' Maru offered.

'No. This time I'm going alone. Just be ready to sail the minute you clap eyes on me.'

He found her tracks soon enough ... running across the soft sand and up into the hills. Jack had been drugged and unconscious for almost six hours, but he didn't think Sovay could be more than an hour ahead of him. She would have had to wait for daylight before attempting to cross the island, and the vegetation was thick, the hills steep and the ground treacherous underfoot. He ran forward in giant strides. For every three imprints that Sovay had made in the sand, he made only one.

At the top of the first hill he paused and took out his telescope. Down below he could see a river and a glittering waterfall lancing down a great shoulder of rock. Some Maori children were playing there, laughing and shrieking as they dived into the water from a row of makeshift rafts. He swung the telescope round. And there was Sovay! She was a little further down the river. She had stolen one of the rafts and was clumsily pushing it out into the water, trusting to the swift current to carry her to the American

119

whaler. Jack whistled softly. It might be easier than continuing on foot. But it would also be a lot more dangerous.

Still, Sovay had set the rules and he had no choice but to follow. Half-running, half-tripping, Jack made his way down the other side of the hill and threw himself into the river, wading through the shallow water. He made no attempt to hide from the children and, seeing him, they cried out in fear and scattered, heading back to their village. Well, by the time they had raised the alarm, he would be a long way away. Jack didn't have time for caution.

He untied a second of the rafts and hoisted himself on to it. There was a long wooden pole lying on top. He used it to push himself away from the bank. A moment later the river had the raft in its grip and he felt himself carried away, propelled round a corner and swept forward, going faster by the minute. There was about half a mile between him and Sovay. All he had to do was stay afloat and he would have her.

The scenery was spectacular now. On both sides of the river the hills zig-zagged up to the sky, turning into mountains as they rose above the trees and bushes. It was as if Jack were trapped in the middle of a fantastic thunderstorm in which the lightning had magically transformed itself into living rock. The river boiled and foamed around him, its water a stampede of white stallions hurling themselves to instant death against the razor-sharp boulders that jutted out from below. The hills soared higher. The river ran faster. Blinded by the spray, twisting and turning, Jack fought to keep control.

And then he heard something that made his

hands tighten automatically on the pole and which had him cursing Sovay under his breath. The roar of the water had intensified. It was deafening, overwhelming. His raft turned another corner. He just had time to see Sovay's raft hit a rock and shatter before his own raft entered the rapids that the river had become, and he found himself fighting for his life.

His raft struck one boulder, then another. Both times Jack managed to soften the impact by using the pole. But a third time he was unlucky. He felt the raft being pulled away from him from beneath. His pole snapped and he lunged forward. A second later he had hit the icy water. Spinning, somer-saulting, drowning, he was pulled along by the river, just managing to gasp for breath before he was underwater again. The rocks were all around him. If he hit one of them, he would break every bone in his body. Jack had never felt so helpless. He was trapped in a blind, freezing, whirling frenzy and he had never been so close to death.

But then he turned another corner. The river slowed down. His head broke through the surface and he breathed fresh air. Using the last of his strength, he swam to the side and dragged himself out on to the bank. He had survived. But where was Sovay? And had she managed to hang on to the pearls?

'Ay sir, it's De Witt's booty. There's no doubt of it.'

The voice came from a clearing a short way away. For a moment Jack wondered if he hadn't hit his head on one of the boulders after all. He had to be dreaming. That sounded like Mr Flack's voice.

'Where's Vincent?'

But that was no dream, nor even a nightmare. It was Anderson. Jack slithered through the grass leaving a watery trail behind him. Poking his head through a hole in the bushes, he looked into the clearing. Anderson was there. The bosun, the surgeon and several of the sailors were with him. And in the middle of the crowd, soaking wet and shivering, Sovay was sitting, her eyes fixed on the bag of pearls that were now in Anderson's hands.

'Where is he?' Anderson repeated.

'Please believe me, sir. As God is my witness I do not know.'

Anderson poured the pearls out of the bag and leant forward, dangling it in front of Sovay's face. 'Where is his ship?'

Sovay stared first at the pearls, then into Anderson's eye. She must have seen some unspoken bargain there. 'Anchored off shore,' she whispered. 'I'll show you.'

'Sensible girl.' Anderson smiled and allowed the pearls to trickle back into the bag. A few minutes later, the procession moved off, Sovay leading the way.

Behind them, the man they were looking for followed.

But getting back was less easy than Sovay thought. The undergrowth was too thick to allow them to follow the river and so they had to strike out across the hills. Soon they were completely lost, and trying to backtrack on themselves only made matters worse. In the hot sun, with mosquitoes buzzing around them and nettles tearing at their legs, tempers frayed and energy was wasted. Then Sovay twisted her ankle.

'You will oblige me, Madam,' Anderson muttered, each word icily polite, 'by walking on.'

'I am not your horse, sir!' Sovay replied. 'And I'll not take one step more until morning — unless you care to carry me.'

Anderson looked around him. His men were tired. He was tired. None of them had ever really recovered from the journey from De Witt's island. He had forced them through sheer willpower to trust their lives once again to the long boat that had brought them there in the first place. That will-power had fed on his hatred of Jack Vincent. He would have gone to sea in a leaking bathtub if he had thought he could catch up with his enemy. They had landed on this island two days ago. There had been no sign of Vincent. He had almost been ready to give up. But then he had found this girl . . .

'Up the 'illside, sir,' the bosun said. 'A cave of some sort.'

Anderson looked up and nodded. It wouldn't do any of them any harm to rest. And if they did come across the *Sea Wolf* the next morning, they would need to be fresh. He nodded and the little party made its way up the hill and into the bosun's cave.

Mr Flack had been carrying a torch and now he lit the way. The cave had been carved out of the rock, though whether by man or nature it was hard to say. The entrance was narrow with a commanding view of the hillside. That suited Anderson.

'Dry . . . and defensible. It'll do.'

One of the sailors wrinkled his nose. 'Smells like the sleeping quarters on the *Success*!' he complained.

'Wood and water, Mr Flack,' Anderson ordered. 'And a guard at the entrance.'

Sovay screamed.

The scream echoed through the cave and everyone jumped. She pointed and Mr Flack turned, holding the torch out in the direction of her finger. There was something there. Or someone. They were not alone in the cave. A figure sat, huddled in the corner, lurking in the shadows. Anderson didn't hesitate. His musket was already primed. He fired. The shot reverberated around the chamber and the figure slumped forward. Anderson took the torch and approached.

'God save us!' the bosun whispered.

Anderson had shot a skeleton. And it wasn't the only one in the cave. There were hundreds of them, sitting with their backs against the rockface, their skulls painted with some sort of red ochre. The cave could have been the antechamber of hell. It had no back but ran, an endless tunnel, into the hill. And everywhere there were bones, yellowing and ancient, some with a few scraps of feather still clinging to them through the years.

'It must be some sort of heathen graveyard,' Anderson muttered.

For one of the sailors, it was too much, whatever it was. Surrounded by the staring, silent crowd, he lost his nerve and ran forward with a thin wail. 'I'm getting out of here!'

'Stop that man!' Anderson snapped. The sailor stopped and looked at him with terrified eyes. 'Dead Maoris harm no one,' Anderson went on. 'And here we'll be safe from any live ones. Get wood and water, Mr Flack, at the double. This is where we're spending the night.'

Jack waited until nightfall before making his

move. Anderson had posted a guard at the mouth of the cave and there was no way he could get in there, but he had noticed something else. The bosun had lit a fire and the smoke was rising out of the ground above the cave, as if through a natural chimney. It was for that point that Jack made now, skirting well round the cave's entrance and making sure he kept out of sight.

He reached the top and looked down. There was a narrow fissure in the ground and through it he could see the glow of Anderson's fire. Holding his breath, he looked closer. The smoke made his eyes water but he could just see Sovay, sitting beside the fire, plucking two game birds. A thick cord tied her ankles. She wouldn't be running anywhere. Jack leant back and sucked in clean air, forcing himself not to cough. Tears were streaming from his eyes, but he was smiling. Soon Anderson and his men would have to sleep. Then Jack would get to work.

In fact Jack slept himself, though only for a few hours. Dawn was approaching when he got to work, collecting as much wild grass as he could carry and stacking it up beside the fissure. The fire was burning low inside the cave, but the flames were still flickering. That was just what Jack wanted. Squinting through the hole to make sure nobody was awake, he began to push the grass through, watching as it span gently in the air and settled on the fire. The grass was damp and at once thick smoke began to belch out, rising up through the ceiling of the cave. But Jack was ready for that too. Now he spread more grass across the fissure, blocking it. The smoke rebounded, filling the cave.

Hastily, he scrambled down the side of the hill.

The sun was just rising, the sky a brilliant shade of pink when the men in the cave began to cough and choke. The guard, who had been half-asleep himself, got to his feet and looked back. It was a mistake. Jack stepped out of the trees and hit him with the barrel of his pistol. The guard slumped. Jack caught him and laid him gently on one side. Then, wrapping a wet handkerchief around his nose and mouth, he went into the cave.

All the men were awake now, their eyes streaming, barely able to draw their breath. They were staggering around the cave like blind men, one unfortunate soldier accidentally walking into a loving embrace with one of the skeletons. Nobody saw Jack. Even if they had they would probably have been too panicked to do anything about it. They were barely conscious, suffocating in the thick smoke. All they wanted to do was to get out — and while Jack stood well back in a jagged cleft, they groped and jostled their way to the entrance.

Jack pushed himself forward and found Sovay. One cut of his knife and she was free. 'Jack . . .!' she shouted.

Jack turned. Anderson was lumbering towards him, reaching out through the smoke. Jack dodged and punched at the same time. His fist caught Anderson on the side of his jaw — a jaw still pock-marked by the exploding musket. Anderson fell face down.

'The pearls . . .?' he demanded.

'In his coat,' Sovay said.

Jack rolled Anderson on to his back and dug his hand into the man's pocket. His fingers closed on the leather pouch and he pulled it out, pocketing it. 'Get out!' he called to Sovay.

Anderson's eyes opened. 'Vincent ...!' he croaked.

Jack ignored him. Despite the wet handkerchief he could barely breathe. Leaving the lieutenant where he lay, he followed Sovay out of the cave. The smoke parted like a curtain. Bright sunlight welcomed him on the other side.

Less welcoming, however, was the Maori war party.

Jack froze. The warriors that he had encountered on the beach stood grouped around the cave. One of Anderson's men had put up a fight and had been killed for it. A horrible wound gaped in the back of his head and thick blood was congealing in a pool around his face. Towers, Mr Flack and the rest were prisoners. Jack kept absolutely still as one of the Maoris stepped forward. He was carrying a 'taiaha' — a hardwood spear with a blade at one end and a feathered handle at the other. Using the taiaha, the warrior flicked the pistol out of his hand.

There was a movement behind him. Anderson had made his way out of the cave. Jack opened his mouth to warn him, but it was too late. The lieutenant had taken in the scene in one second and acted in the next. His hand came up, holding a gun. The taiaha flashed. Anderson screamed and fell to the ground, blood spouting from just below his neck. He was still alive. But the Maori had broken his collar bone.

Slowly, the Maoris closed in on Jack.

'Do something!' Sovay cried out.

Jack opened his mouth. 'Tena koe te rangatira,' he said. 'Tena koutou katoa, e hoa ma. Ko Jack Vincent ahau . . . te kurii o Maru.'

The Maoris stared at him in surprise. Jack hadn't wasted his time with Maru and now he was reminding them that he was their friend, but in their own language. He was probably the only man in the entire South Seas who could have spoken so much and they were visibly impressed. Even so, the chief was still angry. He pointed at the cave with a quivering finger.

'He poukaa rangatira teenei!' he said. 'This is a sacred resting place for our nobles. You have defiled it. You have to die.'

'What's he saying?' Sovay asked.

Jack translated. 'Their ancestors will be angry,' he added. 'They'll demand a sacrifice . . .' He reached into his pocket and took out the leather bag.

'What are you doing?' Sovay whispered.

'A trade . . . I hope.'

Jack took a single pearl out of the bag. It was one of the biggest in the collection and even in their present predicament, Anderson's sailors couldn't help marvelling at it. A man could live for a year on the profits from a pearl like that. The chief, however, was unimpressed. Taking the pearl from Jack he threw it on the ground and stamped on it. Jack picked it up again.

'White man's pounamu!' he said, making exaggerated gestures to accompany his words. 'White man's greenstone! Worth plenty. You take. Trade for guns.' He dug into the bag and took out a whole handful of pearls. He was offering a small fortune, he knew. But what good would a small fortune be to him if he wasn't alive to enjoy it?

'Blood has already been spilt,' he went on, talking again in Maori. 'Kua maringi te toto. All is avenged. God and ancestors can rest easy now.'

The chief considered a moment. His men were still clutching their weapons and Jack knew that the next few seconds would decide their fate. One nod from the old man and they would all be cut to pieces, perhaps served up at the next banquet. The Maoris ate human flesh not just because they needed the meat or liked the taste but because, to them, it was the ultimate revenge. Jack glanced at Anderson who lay groaning on the ground. So much for the feud! It looked as if the two of them would be reunited for ever in death.

But then the chief reached out for the bag and with a shiver of relief Jack gave it to him. The warriors backed away.

Jack turned to the bosun. 'Where's your boat?' he asked.

'A small inlet. A mile or so down the coast.'

'Take Anderson and go. As fast as you can.'

Mr Flack glanced nervously at the Maoris. 'What's to stop them coming after us?'

'Nothing. Just say your prayers and run.'

Two of the sailors leant down and picked up Anderson. The lieutenant was still bleeding. His face was ashen white, but still he tried to speak.

'Save your breath, Harry,' Jack said. 'I know how grateful you are.'

Later that afternoon, Jack and Sovay reached the coast. They were at a point mid-way between the *Sea Wolf* and the American whaler. Here they would go their separate ways. They had said little on the journey. But when they had stopped for water, Jack had plucked a single blossom from a bush and handed it to Sovay. Now she was wearing it in her hair.

'What will you tell Mason and the others?' she asked.

'I'll tell them the truth.'

'That you let me go and gave away all the pearls?' Sovay shook her head. 'They'll cut your throat.'

'I didn't give away all the pearls.' Jack put his hand in his pocket. When he drew it out, there was one pearl nestling on the palm. 'You'd better look after this,' he said.

'Jack . . .'

'It should pay for a passage aboard the American whaler. And there'll be change enough to provide for a new start.' He pressed it into her hand and smiled at her. 'Well, I can hardly divide one pearl between five.'

'We could go together,' Sovay said.

'No, Miss Banks.' He stepped back and bowed. 'Stay out of trouble.'

'I'll do my best.'

He moved away from her, then stopped and turned back for one last time. She was still standing there, gazing at the pearl, his gift to her, a new start. 'Sovay . . .' he called out.

'Yes?'

'You never did say. What did you do? To earn seven years as a convict?'

There was a pause. Then Sovay laughed. 'I'll tell you if we ever meet again, Jack Vincent!'

The sun was setting. Jack walked away, making for the *Sea Wolf*. When he looked back again a few minutes later, Sovay had gone.

9

Not surprisingly, Mason and the others were less than happy to see Jack return empty-handed. He told them what had happened — everything except the fate of the last pearl. But their faces showed doubt and suspicion rather than relief at his close escape.

'How do we know he was captured by Maoris?' Mason asked, shortly after they'd set sail. 'We've only got his word for it. And where are we going now? He never tells us nothing!'

Even Maru was doubtful for once. 'Jack is not a born chief,' he said. 'Maori chiefs listen to the needs of the people. *Then* they tell them what to do.'

Mason sighed. 'With those pearls we could've sailed into London as bold as brass and no one to know who we was.'

'I could see myself bowling down the main street in Limerick,' Pat added. 'In my carriage and pair, me mother at me side, and all the people staring.'

Just then Jack appeared and the three men broke up their conversation abruptly. 'Take the helm, Mason,' Jack ordered.

'Aye, aye, Captain,' Mason said, but there was an ugly note in his voice.

131

They sailed for three days, heading south-west with another good breeze behind them. If Jack was aware of the discontented mutterings of his crew, he didn't show it. Even so, a mood had settled on the *Sea Wolf* that was like a sort of fog. It seeped into everything, its touch cold and clammy and no matter how brightly the sun shone the ship remained locked into a perpetual gloom.

On the third day they spied land.

'Know it, Maru?' Jack asked.

'No.'

Jack glanced at the Maori. Like everyone else on the ship, he seemed to address the captain only in the briefest of monosyllables. 'It's a chance to replenish our water and perhaps find fresh meat.' He grinned, trying to get some reaction from the others. 'Think of it, boys. Nice bit of wild pig. We've had our misfortunes but I've a feeling this island'll bring a change in our luck.'

And for a while it looked as if Jack was right. Mason and Maru lent a willing hand, loading the jolly-boat with the water butts. Pat and Li offered to take the oars.

'De Witt found gold,' Mason reminded them as he heaved the last of the water butts into place. 'He never said where. Maybe we'll find it here.'

Li pushed off. As the jolly-boat turned and began to head towards the island, he smelt something strange in the air. Pat smelt it too.

'Queer smell,' Pat muttered. 'Like sulphur.'

'Dragon . . .' Li said, suddenly grim.

'So it's true, then?' Pat asked. 'You have dragons in China?'

'Oh, yes. A dragon's belch is the sound of thunder. The wind from his belly makes the typhoons.

Lightning flashes from his nostrils and his breath is hotter than a forest fire.' The smell of sulphur was stronger now. It hung in a blanket over the entire island, smothering any sound. Even the waves were silent. Li's face was full of foreboding. 'Dragon Island . . .' he whispered.

Jack left Li and Pat to fill the water butts and struck out on his own. There was something about the island that he didn't like, something strangely menacing. To look at, it was like any other of the South Sea islands he had visited. The vegetation was thick and tropical, sprouting all round the hills which rose above. This island was volcanic — that would explain the smell. But there was something else. Jack felt as if he were surrounded by poison. Open his mouth at the wrong time, stretch out and touch the wrong plant . . . it was as if there were a hundred different ways to die.

He was about half a mile from the beach. The trees had thinned out but a light mist had risen up as if to fill the gaps. Something moved. Jack blinked, the sun in his eyes. It looked like a man . . . but a man who leapt like a goat. Had he imagined it? The figure sprang again, launching himself from one rock to another.

'Hey!' Jack shouted. 'You there! Stop!'

The man ignored him.

Jack tried again in Maori. 'Tatari, e hoa ma Tatari!'

The man bounded away. Without hesitating, Jack followed him, plunging into the mist which became thicker with every step he took. Now he could barely see anything. Everything was white. But then he had burst through to the other side.

He stopped and stared. He had somehow stepped into another world.

It was beautiful. Paradise. He was in a miniature grotto, surrounded by tumbling waterfalls of turquoise, saffron and brilliant green. Steam rose out of pools in luminescent clouds. Silvery rock enclosed the grotto, reflecting the colours and intensifying them. Even the sky, seen through a soft pink haze, seemed suffused with a light that had come from somewhere other than the sun.

And in the middle of it all stood a man who could have stepped out of 'Robinson Crusoe' — or the Bible perhaps. There was something of the prophet in him, especially in his eyes, bright and unfocused, and in his wild, straggling hair and beard. But his clothes, made from animal skins, were those of a castaway. There were ten more men behind him, all equally unreal. It almost looked as if they had been waiting for Jack to arrive.

'Good morning!' the man said. 'Ben Frobisher, lord of this island, erstwhile mate of the *Dolphin*.'

'Jack Vincent . . .'

'From the ship in the bay?'

'Yes.'

'I'm pleased to meet you.' The castaway (if that's what he was) gave Jack a friendly smile. 'This is John Herrick, the bosun.'

A middle-aged man stepped forward. 'Pleased to meet you,' he said.

Jack shook hands. The bosun was quite different to Ben Frobisher. He was younger, with a frank, honest face. His eyes met Jack's. The other man's seemed to look right through him.

'And these are the surviving seamen from our ship,' Frobisher went on. 'Luckily for us, the ship

134

struck on a reef some ten years back.'

'Luckily?' Jack said.

'Luckily.' Frobisher smiled and brought his hands together as if in prayer. 'We have heard the word and we have understood.' As Jack stared at him in disbelief, he gestured at the geyser behind him. 'Malachi has shown us the way,' he intoned. 'He seldom speaks, but when he does it is to announce an event of great importance. Today he has given us a ship.'

'Given you a ship?' Jack didn't like the sound of that.

'Your crew will make room for us,' Frobisher explained. Suddenly his voice changed. 'I expect you're hungry,' he said. 'We fixed up some grub the moment we spotted your sail. Not a banquet, but a long sight better than ship's tack and salt pork, I'll be bound. If you'll follow me . . .'

Jack followed his host further into the grotto. The ten shipwrecked sailors went in with him. It was all quite remarkable. Ben Frobisher had two separate identities, and two voices to go with them.

'Malachi has shown us the way . . .' That was the prophet.

'We fixed up some grub . . .' The shipwrecked sailor.

Unfortunately, Jack couldn't help feeling that they added up to one man who was completely insane.

The survivors of the *Dolphin* had built themselves an encampment high up on a plateau near the volcanic pools. The *Dolphin* itself figured largely in it, for the timbers from the wrecked ship had been used to build a large communal hall.

135

The ribbing from the ship had been upturned and planted all round the building which gave it the look of a temple. The impression was heightened by an inscription burnt into a cross beam above the door: HIS ANGER POURS OUT LIKE A STREAM OF FIRE. THE ROCKS MELT BEFORE HIM. Presumably, Jack thought, this was where Frobisher worshipped his Malachi — or Mallarky, as he pronounced it.

'Of course, it's been rough, Captain,' Frobisher was saying as they entered the hall. 'But we had one stroke of luck. We found goats on the island.'

'You've done very well,' Jack said.

'Not well enough.' Frobisher shook his head. 'We lost three of our men.'

'I'm sorry.'

'They sinned. They could not find the way.'

He had become a prophet again. Jack looked at his host uneasily, determining to get back to the *Sea Wolf* the moment he could.

There was a raised dais at the far end of the hall with a table running across it. Frobisher led Jack here and sat down on his right hand side. Christ and Saint Peter, Jack thought to himself, but he smiled politely and said nothing. In the meantime, one of the seamen had filled two cups with some sort of brew. He gave one to Frobisher, one to Jack.

'Try it, Captain,' Frobisher said. 'We call it Malachi's grog. It's made from dried fungus and all kinds of herbs which we've found on the island. It sustains us in our misfortune. It strengthens us in our purpose.'

Jack waited until Ben had drunk his own 'grog' before he did the same. Then he took a cautious sip. Although he somehow doubted that it would

136

sustain him in any misfortune, he had to admit that it tasted surprisingly good. He drank all that he had been given, then held out his cup for more.

Frobisher got to his feet. 'His anger pours out in a stream of fire!' he called out to the seamen in the voice of the prophet.

'The rocks melt before him,' the seamen chorused.

'The day comes glowing like a furnace.'

'And on that day the evil-doers shall be cast into the burning pit.'

Suddenly the hall was silent and all eyes were on Jack. It was as if they expected him to say something and he felt he ought not to disappoint them. He was standing up, which was strange because he couldn't remember getting to his feet.

'Well ...' he said. 'Thank you, Mr Frobisher. But now if you'll excuse me ...'

He was going to leave. But his feet wouldn't move. He looked down and saw that roots had sprung out of his toes, snaking into the ground. He was stuck fast, like a tree. No. That wasn't possible ...

'Excuse me ... Excuse me ... My crew ...'

The hall was glowing red. He could hear his own voice but it didn't seem to be coming from him. It was a long way away. And he was sweating. Why was that? His teeth began to chatter.

'His anger pours out like a stream of fire ...'

They were Frobisher's words. But Frobisher had gone. Jack was in the heart of a volcano. He wanted to scream, but he could only laugh. He was in the heart of a volcano and it was erupting all around him. The whole world was red. Molten lava poured on to him.

'The earth seethes. Those who lose the way

shall be cast into the burning pit . . .'

That was Frobisher again. It was good to hear his voice. Jack was on the edge of a great lake now. A lake of boiling mud. A jet of steam broke through the surface and leapt out like a hissing snake.

'Hear the words of Malachi! He calls you. He shows you the way through the mists of ignorance. Malachi sees all . . .'

Oh yes. He was flying now. Flying with Malachi. And what was that down there . . . so small? Laughing, Jack recognized the *Sea Wolf*, floating like a toy ship far down in the bay. But then Malachi took him. Malachi saw everything. Together they plunged down until he could see Mason, Pat, Maru and Li. They were talking about him. Of course they were. Jack knew what they thought of him. But he hadn't known what they were plotting.

'We don't need him,' Li was saying.

'I can navigate,' declared Maru.

'Leave him to stew on his island, I say.' Pat drove his knife into the deck.

'I'll cut his throat and feed him to the sharks.' Mason plucked the knife out again and waved it in the air.

In the air. Jack was flying for a second time. Breaking through the clouds. And on the other side of the clouds . . .? He was back in the hall. Back with Frobisher and the others. He was still standing on the dais. He knew now that he had been drugged. The brew he had been given . . . he could taste it in his mouth. But it wasn't like the drug that Sovay had slipped into his food. He liked this drug. He wanted more.

'We shall build a new world from the ashes of

the old,' Ben Frobisher said. 'A world without vice, without war. I trust you will join us in our mission, Captain Vincent?'

'Malachi shall guide us on our way,' Jack said.

'He's been gone a long time,' Mason muttered, sitting on the deck of the *Sea Wolf*, stitching a sail.

'Anything could have happened to him,' Pat said.

Li put down his corner of the sail. 'Perhaps it would be in our best interests to go ashore and conduct a small search,' he suggested. He looked up. Maru was leaning against the rail, holding a small clump of mushrooms that he had found on the island. He had been silent and moody ever since he had come upon them. 'What do you think, Maru?' Li asked.

'I am thinking many things . . .' Maru crushed the mushrooms in the palms of his hand and scattered the pieces on the sea.

A moment later a figure appeared on the beach, his hands raised, waving frantically.

'It's Jack!' Pat exclaimed.

All three of them leapt up and joined Maru at the railing. Jack was shouting something. It was difficult to hear at first, but then his words reached them across the great expanse of water.

'Gold! The island's made of gold!'

Mason gave a great whoop. 'I told you!' he yelled. 'Didn't I tell you! We're rich, my hearties!'

'Come on!' Pat almost fell over in his hurry to get to the jolly-boat. Li was right behind him. But Maru hung back. 'What's the problem, Maru?' Pat demanded.

Maru glanced at the fragments of mushroom,

still floating around the ship. 'Bad spirits . . .' he muttered.

Li laughed. Pat and Mason ignored him. Rowing as hard as they could, they pulled for the shore. Alone on the *Sea Wolf*, Maru watched them go. He saw them greeted by Jack. Jack pointed at something and they ran across the beach, disappearing round the other side. Then they were gone. Maru stayed where he was, his eyes fixed on the beach. A moment later, Jack returned. He got into the jolly-boat and rowed himself out to the *Sea Wolf*.

Maru waited for him. He was afraid. He had seen the mushrooms before. He knew what they could do to a man.

Jack climbed over the side of the *Sea Wolf*. But was it Jack? It was the same face, the same voice. But they were the eyes of another creature. Dragon eyes. 'I want you ashore with the others, Maru,' he said.

'You . . . you're not Jack Vincent.'

'Don't play the fool!'

'Ko porangi koe!' Maru broke into Maori. 'You're not Jack. You're a kehua . . . evil spirit.'

Jack raised his musket. Maru charged. The gun went off, missing him by inches. And then he had reached Jack, throwing himself on top of him, wrestling him to the deck.

But the gun had reached other ears.

As Maru fought, he became aware that he was no longer alone. Other figures were climbing over the side of the boat, men with the same dragon eyes. Breaking free of Jack, he picked up the musket by the barrel and swung it like a war-club. It made contact with one of the men's stomachs. The man collapsed groaning. Maru swung it again.

But they were all around him now. Somebody hit him from behind. Maru's legs buckled beneath him. The last thing he saw was Jack Vincent, a cruel smile on his face, pointing at him. Then he was out.

When he woke up he was on dry land. His face was pressed against the sand. There was sand in his mouth. He groaned and spat it out.

'Good at betraying folks, ain't you, Vincent?'

Maru recognized Mason's voice. He opened his eyes and saw Mason, Li and Pat, tied up on the sand. Jack was standing in front of them. The Jack that wasn't Jack.

'Seek out Malachi . . .' he said. 'Search out the way!'

'He's off his head!' Mason growled.

'The day comes glowing like a furnace. On that day the evil-doers shall be cast into the burning pit.'

'It is not Captain . . .' Maru tried to sit up on the sand. That was when he found that his own hands and legs were bound. 'It is kehua. Devil man!'

Jack ignored him. Another man had called to him. 'I'm coming, Ben,' he said.

Maru, Li, Mason and Pat watched Jack stride off down the beach. They watched him get back into the jolly-boat and sail out to the *Sea wolf* where the rest of Frobisher's men were waiting. They saw the ship raise anchor and drift away. And they were still watching, helpless, when it was only a dot on the horizon.

By the time they managed to get out of their bonds, it was too late. The *Sea Wolf* had gone. They were marooned.

10

The *Sea Wolf* made slow progress to begin with. The crew, used to their life on the island, had almost forgotten how to handle a ship. The bosun would have been glad to have taken a rope to them to get them moving, but Frobisher had other ideas.

'A tot of Malachi's grog — that'll liven them up!' he declared. 'Bosun, a tot for each man to toast the success of our mission.'

After that, the ship made better progress, sailing due north and retracing its path towards Anderson's island. Jack was still, nominally, the captain of the *Sea Wolf*. But Frobisher was its master.

'The Channel . . .' he said on that first afternoon as he studied the charts with Jack and the bosun. 'That's the hub. Set course for the English Channel. Westward round the Horn, then up through the Atlantic.'

Jack looked doubtful. Now that his mind was busily occupied in plotting the ship's course, some of the drug's effect had worn off. 'She's a small ship, Mr Frobisher,' he said. 'I doubt she'll weather the Horn.'

'Malachi will still the raging ocean,' Frobisher, the prophet, intoned.

'He'll have a hard task around Tierra del Fuego,' Jack remarked.

'Heresy! You stray from the path, Captain . . .'

For a moment it looked as if Frobisher were going to turn on Jack, but just then the door opened and a sailor came in with three mugs. Frobisher lifted his in a toast.

'To our mission!' he said. 'Peace. Prosperity. And brotherhood!'

He drained his mug in one. Jack did the same. But unseen by either of the others, the bosun hesitated and when the ship rolled he lurched forward, spilling his tot on the deck. It was an exaggerated gesture. Losing the drug had definitely not been an accident . . .

'North-east, Mr Frobisher,' Jack cried, his fervour returning. 'That should be our course! Through the Coral Sea and on to the Dutch Indies, spreading the word as we go. To India, then Persia, through the land of the Ottoman Turks, and on into Greece. It's the route of Alexander the Great.'

'Alexander the Great!' Frobisher drew himself up to his full height (which wasn't, in fact, very high).

Jack poured himself another tot of the grog. For a moment he swayed over the chart. Then his finger lunged down to stab at a tiny island. 'Our first landfall!' he said. It was Anderson's island.

'It's small,' Frobisher remarked.

'It's a beginning,' Jack countered.

'Is it populous?'

'Do numbers count?' Jack threw back his second tot. 'On that island is a man whose stiff-necked pride must be rooted out. He and his whole company of evil-doers shall be burnt like chaff. It is the will of Malachi.'

143

'Are there none to be saved?' Frobisher asked.
'None.'

The second tot of grog had an unfortunate effect on Jack.

It began with a dream, a replay of everything he had been through, seen through the eye of an exploding volcano. There was Anderson, laughing at him as he received his fifty lashes on board the *Success*. There was Anderson, torturing him with the sight of water when he was tied up to the mast in the stockade. And suddenly Anderson was on board the *Sea Wolf*. He had burst out of one of the hatches and was standing there, on the deck.

Jack no longer knew if he was dreaming or awake. Reality and hallucination had become one. His enemy was there. He had to be destroyed. Drawing his cutlass, he charged out of the cabin, shouting.

Two deck hands ran forward as they saw Jack appear. They tried to stop him but he just shrugged them off. Why were they staring at him like that? Couldn't they see that his old enemy had come back and that the feud demanded an end?

Jack slashed down with the cutlass. There was the clang of metal hitting metal and his whole arm shuddered. So it wasn't an illusion. He thrust forward again, trying to pin Anderson against the bulwarks. Out of the corner of his eye, he saw the bosun leave the wheel and run towards him, his face full of alarm. Left alone, the wheel span and the ship yawed. Overhead, the sails were thundering in the wind. A huge wave tilted the *Sea Wolf* just as Jack aimed another blow at

Anderson. But for the wave he would have killed him. Instead he staggered back only to be grabbed by the bosun. At the same time, both men lost their balance. Jack crashed into the deck, his cutlass flying. Something hit his head. When he opened his eyes again, he saw what he had done.

He had been fighting Ben Frobisher. The drug had confused him, played tricks with him. Anderson wasn't there. He never had been. If the bosun hadn't reached him in time he would have cut the Priest of Malachi into several pieces.

Frobisher was not amused. 'Cast him into the ocean!' he commanded.

'Sir?' The bosun got to his feet.

'He has lost the path.'

'Give him time, sir.' The bosun looked apologetically at Jack. 'We gave the others time, sir,' he went on. 'Them that lost their way. It was seven days before they was cast into the pit.'

The other seamen muttered their agreement, but Frobisher looked doubtful. He had almost been killed. Beads of sweat clung to his forehead, and his eyes, wild to begin with, bulged in their sockets.

'It ain't easy, sir,' the bosun went on, 'finding the way to Malachi . . .'

'Very well!' Frobisher barked. 'Seven days. Put him in irons and throw him into the hold.' He took one last thoughtful look at Jack. 'But make sure he gets his ration of Malachi grog . . .'

But Jack never touched another drop of the poisonous brew.

He had been aware, somewhere in the back of his mind, that the grog was responsible for something he couldn't understand. It affected his

145

mind, the same way it had affected Frobisher and
the others ... and it was all the more deadly
because it seemed so pleasant. When he was with
them it had been impossible to fight the drug.
Now that he was alone he brought all his will-
power to resist it. He knew that although you
began by taking the drug, the drug ended up
taking you.

And so whenever he was given his ration he
poured it away. He thought of it as something
sent by Anderson — sometimes even as Anderson himself. It was easier that way. All the
hatred that he felt for his old enemy he directed at
the drug, until he could no longer bear even to
look at it. And in the days that followed, as the
Sea Wolf sailed ever further on its journey, he
gradually won back his sanity.

Meanwhile, Frobisher kept a careful check on
his errant disciple. Every day the bosun would
carry down his ration of grog and every day
Frobisher would ask, 'Is he taking his grog?'

'Yes, sir.'

'Will he find the path?'

'Oh yes, sir.'

'Good!' Frobisher smiled, his eyes gleaming. 'I
want him with us when we make landfall. This
island was his idea. He will share in our triumph.'

'And what happens if it isn't a triumph, sir?'

'Then he perishes in the ocean!'

Every day the bosun told Frobisher what he
wanted to hear and every day Frobisher believed
him. But as Jack emerged from the mists of con-
fusion and madness into which the drug had propelled him, he noticed that there was something
strange about John Herrick. He spoke of Malachi
and the path, just like the others, but there was

146

something unconvincing about him, as if . . .

'You're *not* mad!' Jack exclaimed on the third day of his imprisonment.

The bosun blinked. 'No, sir.'

'You saved my life when I attacked Frobisher. The others are all crazy, but you're not. Why not?'

The bosun looked fearfully over his shoulder. 'I'm a'feared, sir,' he whispered. 'If they catch us, they'll kill us.'

'Just tell me . . .'

'I went along with them,' the bosun began, '. . . at the start anyway. But I'm a God-fearing man, sir, and when I saw what the grog was doing, when I saw them cast three poor devils into the boiling mud, I ran into the forest. I found a cave and hid in it, sir, until the grog had lost its hold. It weren't easy, sir, as you'll know.'

'Then you went back?'

'Yes, and talked their mumbo-jumbo and joined in their wicked goings-on. But I didn't take the grog. Not for ten years.'

'Ten years!' Jack stared at the other man through the gloom. 'You've kept this up for ten years!'

'And I doubt if I'll be able to keep it up much longer. Sooner or later they'll find me out and kill me, like they killed the others.'

Once again the bosun glanced towards the hatch, terrified of being overheard. Jack held out his manacled hands. 'Set me free, Bosun,' he hissed. 'Then there'll be two of us . . .'

'I durst not.' The bosun shook his head.

'It's our only chance.'

'No, sir. No!'

The bosun backed away, still shaking his head.

147

Ten years with Frobisher had been too much for him. Ten years playing a lunatic game with a horrible death always looming over him . . . the man was close to breaking. A moment later he was gone. Jack lowered his hands. Mr Herrick might not be willing to help him yet. But surely the time would come.

The next day they reached Anderson's island.

'If they are evil-doers, they shall be rooted out. And you, Captain Vincent, you who brought us here, shall have the honour of being the first man ashore.'

There were eight of them in the jolly-boat. Frobisher was at the front with Jack beside him. Then came the bosun and behind him, pulling at the oars, six men from the *Sea Wolf*, all armed. Jack gazed ahead of them. He could see the stockade that Anderson, and De Witt before him, had occupied.

But the Union Jack wasn't flying and there was nobody in sight. Jack felt a slight fluttering of unease. He had led Frobisher and his men to the island when the drug had had him in its grip. What would they do if they found it was empty?

The jolly-boat crunched on to the beach. Jack's hands were still manacled and he swayed as he climbed out. The bosun caught hold of him and he felt something cold and hard being pressed into the palm of his hand. Nobody else noticed anything. But when he straightened up he was holding a key.

'Spread out,' Jack said.

Frobisher and his men began to fan out across the beach. All Jack's senses were alert. Any minute now he expected Anderson to open fire.

148

But still everything was silent. He reached the gate of the stockade and pushed it. It swung open.

'Anderson!' Jack called. No answer. 'Anderson . . . it's Vincent!'

But the stockade was empty. A scrap of paper had been pinned to the mast, its corners already yellowing in the open air. Jack walked across and plucked it off.

'Read it,' Frobisher said. His voice was cold.

'After being cast away by mutineers,' Jack read, 'I have embarked this day on the merchantman *Artemis*, under Captain Beckett. It is my duty to search out Jack Vincent and his fellow convicts and bring them to the gallows. Signed, Lieutenant H. Anderson.'

Jack finished the message. Frobisher stared at him. Jack smiled, then began to laugh. So Anderson had slipped away again! Frobisher, however, was less amused.

'Viper with a silken tongue!' he roared. 'You have led us from the path, used false words to lure us into the wilderness. You shall be stamped into the dust, burnt up like a tangle of briars. Your bones shall be cast on the barren mountain to be gnawed by wolves and jackals. Seize him!'

Three of the seamen closed in on Jack who was still laughing at the empty stockade and its farewell message. But even as he laughed his mind was at work. He knew this was the right moment, perhaps the only chance he would have to get away. His eyes never leaving Frobisher's, he turned the key in the manacles then slipped his hand out.

The seamen were getting closer. Frobisher opened his mouth to speak. Grasping the chains in both hands, Jack swung them and hit him full in the face.

The prophet was knocked off his feet. The seamen stopped in their tracks as if they had felt the full force of the blow themselves. Someone had struck their master! It was impossible! How could the great Malachi have allowed it?

Jack was already running for the gate. One of the seamen stood between him and it. The man was already lifting his musket, bringing it round to aim at Jack. He would never make it.

But then the bosun swung an arm, knocking the musket away. The seaman fired but the shot went wild, narrowly missing Frobisher himself who howled with fear and anger.

'Come on!' Jack shouted.

The bosun had committed himself. There could be no turning back now, no further pretence. With the seamen close on their heels, the two of them fled from the stockade and ran for the cover of the woods.

They ran until the sweat was pouring from their faces. Jack's heart was thundering in his chest and he could barely catch breath.

'Got to rest . . .!' he panted, throwing himself to the ground. 'Too long in the hold . . .'

The bosun was not much fitter. Gratefully he sank to his knees. Frobisher's men were a long way behind them now, thundering off in the wrong direction.

'Twice . . .' Jack gulped.

'Twice what?'

'Twice you . . . saved my life.'

'Yes. But for how long?'

As the sun set that evening, Ben Frobisher raised a mug of Malachi's grog. He and his men were sitting around a bonfire in the centre of the com-

150

pound, but now there was something very different about him. It wasn't just the great bruise looping mauve and yellow across his face. It wasn't just the bandage slanting down above his eyes. It was his voice. The prophet in him seemed to have been knocked out. Only a madman was left.

'We have them trapped,' he cackled. 'At first light we'll comb the island, every inch of it. They have no food, no muskets. So if we don't find them, we'll starve them. Then we'll get on with our mission.'

The seamen looked at him unenthusiastically. Malachi had let them down twice in one day. They were beginning to wonder if Malachi was everything he was cracked up to be.

'I want two men patrolling the beach,' he went on. 'Two men on the ship, and the jolly-boat to ride at her stern. They'll not escape, damn them! I'll have them spread-eagled and fed to the crabs.'

He raised the mug and drank it in one. His men followed suit. And as darkness fell and the night wind blew softly through the stockade, the drug coursed through their blood sending them on their whirling journey through the land of make-believe.

Frobisher woke up in the middle of the night.

For a moment he thought he was still dreaming — a horrible dream about some sort of creature that had come out of the forest to grab him. Then he realized with a shudder of horror that although he was awake, the creature was still there. He could hear it. And it was getting closer.

He ran out of his cabin and into the stockade. Outside the noise was louder and even more terrible. It was a sort of ghostly yowling that seemed to vibrate in the air. No human had ever made that sound . . . nor any animal that Frobisher had ever seen. The yowling became a shriek. Despite himself, Frobisher looked over his shoulder convinced that he would see some impossible monster come hurtling towards him. There was nothing there. But the shriek rose in pitch, stretching out to fill the very sky.

The other seamen were out in the open, huddled round the fire. One of them threw a log on to it and a twist of brilliant red sparks rose upwards. They were terrified. Frobisher could see it at once and he knew that even Malachi would seem less dreadful to them than this invisible animal.

'It's just some wild animal,' he called out to them. 'Probably jackals howling over Vincent's bones.'

He spoke the words lightly, almost like a joke. But then the howling became louder still. The men panicked. As the flames leapt up they were on their feet and running out of the compound, into the night . . . leaving Frobisher shouting and cursing them, but for the first time in ten long years, alone.

It had been Jack's idea.

It was a bull-roarer. In England it was nothing more than a toy, a piece of wood on the end of a string. You whirled it round your head and it somehow caught the wind and made the most terrifying sound. But the Maoris had another name for it. They called it a 'purerehua' and used it in their rituals. Listening to it now he could understand why. It was as if the devil had been set loose on the island.

He had cut the bull-roarer from a piece of wood, using the bosun's knife. The bosun was swinging it now, spinning the wood on a length of creeper. And Frobisher's men were all over the place.

'The island's haunted . . .'

'Demons . . .'

'Spirits . . .'

'Malachi has forsaken us . . .'

The disembodied words drifted through the night across the water and out to the *Sea Wolf* where the two seamen that Frobisher had posted as guards stood, wondering what all the fuss was about.

They never saw Jack pulling himself out of the water behind them. One moment they were leaning over the railings. The next they were spluttering and splashing in the water wishing now, when it was too late, that they had learnt how to swim.

Meanwhile, back on the island, Frobisher had managed to calm down his men.

'Get brands from the fire,' he commanded. 'We'll scour the beach. We'll set the forest ablaze. Malachi will protect us!'

Jack heard him. Already he had left the *Sea Wolf* and was rowing back towards the shore to collect the bosun.

'This way! Follow me!'

Forcing down the first stirrings of panic, Jack realized that the bull-roarer's use was almost over. It had scared the men. It was still making a fearsome noise. But no monster had appeared. Nothing had come out of the darkness. They were rallying around Frobisher.

And then the bosun had reached the jolly-boat, wading out into the sea. He flung the bull-roarer away from him. There was a distant splash and silence returned to the night.

'Quick . . .!' Jack whispered.

'Stop them!' Frobisher screamed.

The bosun had helped turn the boat round. Jack was pulling away with all his strength. He was facing the shore, looking over the bosun's shoulder as the other man climbed in with him. He saw Frobisher run down to the very edge of the water and take out his musket. He saw the flash as he fired. The bosun jerked forward, his eyes wide with shock. Then he fell back into the water.

'Bosun . . .!' Jack called out.

But the bosun was dead. The jolly-boat shot away.

On the shore, Frobisher threw down the gun, powerless to stop Jack from reaching the *Sea Wolf*. He was stuck on another island with all his men. The great mission had failed before it had even begun.

'The curses of Malachi fall on you!' he screamed. 'May he damn you in hell! May the crows tear out your liver and the maggots feed on . . .'

But Jack had already reached the *Sea Wolf*. He had cut the anchor loose and set sail.

The curses of Malachi fell on an empty sea.

11

Exactly one week had passed since Maru, Mason, Pat and Li had been left stranded on Ben Frobisher's island. They had managed to untie themselves eventually and they at least had no problems finding food and water (although they kept well clear of the island's mushrooms). But not an hour had gone past without one of them scanning the horizon, looking out for the sails of a ship.

And the morning after Jack Vincent had defeated the disciples of Malachi, even as he turned the *Sea Wolf* southwards and sailed her single-handedly back to rescue his friends, Maru spotted a sail.

For a while the four men stood on the beach, simply staring at it. Although none of them had ever mentioned it, they all knew that Frobisher and his castaways had spent ten long years on the island. That a boat should have appeared in only seven days was nothing short of a miracle.

They stared at it, then, with a sort of awe. It was almost as if they didn't believe it was there. At last Pat broke the silence.

'Ah what a grand sight it is!' he exclaimed. 'Like a beautiful angel of mercy!'

Mason snatched the telescope from him and

held it up to his eye. 'A merchantman?' he muttered. 'A whaler maybe — what d'you think?'

'I think we should light a signal fire,' Li said. 'Otherwise what it is will forever remain conjecture.'

'While we remain here!' Pat added.

'Then get going, you idle Irish ninny!' Mason shouted.

The thought of the ship sailing by galvanized all four of them into action. Li and Pat furiously piled up brushwood while Mason, equally furiously, shouted at them. At the same time, Maru practised the delicate art of 'hika ahi', or fire-making, rubbing together a flat board and a pointed stick and chanting excitedly all the while.

Meanwhile, the ship sailed closer, its sails billowing, the sun glinting off its polished stanchions.

The four of them might have been a little less energetic if they had known the ship's name. It was the *Artemis*, and Anderson was on board.

He was standing on deck with the captain — a tough, weather-beaten man called Beckett. Beckett had the sort of eyes that could tell a few stories and the sort of mouth that almost certainly wouldn't, at least not to anyone he didn't know and trust. He was dressed in rough, dirty clothes, his ample stomach hanging over the band of his trousers. He hadn't shaved that morning. Stubble clung to his chin like moss.

He was the complete opposite of Anderson who had, in truth, changed little since his days on the *Success*. Anderson's uniform was faded now and had been patched in more than one place, but he still wore it like an officer of the Royal Navy, pulling it tight over his rapidly shrinking frame and never forgetting to polish what few buttons were left. He still stood erect, never letting anyone forget that he had once held a position of command and would one day do so again. There was one other difference between the two men. Beckett was cheerful. Anderson was morose.

'I made a promise,' he was saying. 'I intend to keep it.'

'Ah yes!' Beckett smiled. 'The ringleader. What's his name again?'

'Vincent.' He spat the word out as if it were poison in his mouth. 'I promised him I would track him down, and God help me, I will!'

It wasn't the first time that Anderson and Beckett had had this conversation. In fact, Beckett often remarked, the man could think of nothing else. He was fanatical, obsessed. Jack Vincent, Jack Vincent, Jack Vincent . . . Beckett was almost beginning to wish he had left the lieutenant back on his island.

'Why risk your life to hang a man?' he asked now. 'It's madness. Besides, if he's got a Maori with him he's more likely to end up as someone's dinner. They're warriors — all of 'em. And they don't think that much of pakehas . . . unless they're served up like a mutton roast.'

Just then there was a cry from one of the sailors and Anderson rushed over to the side of the boat. They were passing yet another of the islands and faint now, but getting thicker every moment, smoke was rising upwards from the beach.

'It's a signal!' Anderson said.

'From whom?' Beckett's voice was sarcastic. 'Your convict friends?'

Anderson nodded. 'Almost certainly.'

'You're obsessed with convicts, man. It's just a fire — that's all.'

'You're wrong.' Anderson gazed at Beckett, and not for the first time the captain saw the glimmer of madness in his eyes. 'It's a signal.'

'What if it is?' Beckett was unwilling to change course. 'You can't be sure it's being made by white men. It could be a trick to lure us inshore.'

'I thought you were friendly with the Maoris,' Anderson said.

'I am. But which Maoris? The Ngapuhi? The Ngati Miru? The Tainui? We're not talking about a nation. They're warring tribes fighting among themselves. And they're very slippery customers too, I can tell you.'

Anderson slammed a fist down against the gunwale. 'I'll stake my life it's the convicts,' he cried. 'Perhaps even Vincent himself.'

Beckett gazed back at Anderson with a mixture of amusement and intrigue. The man was mad, of course. But just how mad ...? 'Very well,' he said. 'We'll take a closer look, just for your satisfaction. But every man who goes on shore has a musket. And I'm priming the cannons, too.'

Mason saw the jolly-boat launched from the *Artemis* and ran forward with a whoop of joy. Pat performed an impromptu jig on the sand. Maru muttered excitedly in Maori, and even Li was bouncing on his heels, beaming extravagantly. When the jolly-boat reached the beach they were waiting to greet it.

Then Anderson stepped out.

The smile faded from Mason's lips and Pat felt

158

his heart sink into his stomach. Li had never seen Anderson before, but he knew at once that their rescue was less of a miracle than they had all thought. Anderson was holding a gun. It was too late to do anything. In seconds they were surrounded.

'Where's Vincent?' Anderson demanded. Nobody spoke. 'Where is he?'

'Gone.' Pat muttered the one word sullenly. 'Left us here to die.'

'You lying scum!' Anderson noticed Li for the first time. 'Who's this?' he asked.

Li tiptoed forward and bowed, holding both hands together. He had summed up the situation in seconds. This man was dangerous. It was too early to say what he was planning, but for now it might be better to act innocently. 'Me velly good cook, sir,' he said, putting a caricature of a Chinese accent into his voice.

'Where's Vincent?'

Li shrugged.

Beckett had been in the boat with Anderson. Now he stepped forward and addressed Maru. 'E moohio ana koe kei hea ia?' he asked in fluent Maori. 'Do you know where he is?'

'He's gone,' Maru replied, also in Maori. 'He took the boat and went. They're telling the truth.'

'Well?' Anderson snapped.

'He says the same,' Beckett assured him. 'Vincent left 'em here.'

'They're lying.'

'Then where's his boat?'

Anderson ground his foot into the sand and flushed with rage. 'I'll make them tell . . .'

Beckett looked at him, mildly disgusted. The

man was behaving like a sadistic schoolboy. 'I've wasted enough time,' he growled. 'We'll take the three of them back to the boat. But not the Maori. I'm not having him aboard.'

'Why not?' Anderson demanded.

'Because I trade with these people and I'm not spoiling any trust I've built up by taking one of 'em prisoner, that's why!'

'But he'll warn . . .'

'He stays here!'

'What about Vincent?'

'To hell with Vincent!'

For a moment it looked as if the two men were going to hurl themselves at each other's throats. Then Beckett forced himself to calm down. 'Listen, Anderson,' he said in a more reasonable voice. 'When I finish what I'm here for, I'll take you, your crew and your prisoners to Norfolk Island as I promised. But I'm not going on a wild goose chase. Do you understand?' He threw his musket to one of the seamen and turned back to the jolly-boat. 'Take 'em to the boat!' he called out. Then he waved at Maru. 'Haere ra, e te rangatira! Goodbye, Chief . . .'

Beckett climbed into the boat. Mason, Pat and Li were led in after him. Anderson followed, white with anger. Maru watched as the other seamen climbed in and then pulled away, carrying the prisoners back to the boat. He shook his head. These pakehas! Couldn't they ever agree on anything?

Jack Vincent arrived back at the island later that same day.

Maru saw the *Sea Wolf* reappear from the top of a hill and climbed down to the other side of the

160

island to greet it. He didn't however, rush out with open arms. While Jack launched his own jolly-boat and rowed in, Maru crept through the under-growth, keeping out of sight. While Jack walked across the sand, calling out their names, Maru crouched down, every muscle coiled. Finally Jack reached him. Maru sprang. Taken by surprise, Jack fell back into the sand with Maru's hands clenched tightly around his throat. He opened his mouth to shout, but could not draw breath. With a soundless curse he slashed down, breaking Maru's grip and pulled himself to his feet.

'Hold it, man!' he croaked before Maru could attack again. 'I came back for you. See? No devil. I'm clean!' Desperately he searched through his head for the Maori word for clean. 'Noa!' he shouted. 'Noa — see?'

Jack held out his hands, palms upwards, a ges-ture of entreaty. Maru looked into his eyes. It was true. The kehua, devil-man, was gone. The eyes were clear. They were the eyes of his friend.

'Ke tika!' Maru said, nodding. 'Good.'

'Where are the others?' Jack asked.

Maru's face darkened again. Slowly, he began to tell the tale.

Beckett held a match to his pipe and puffed, his cheeks glowing red as they reflected the flame. The remains of a good meal littered the table in front of him . . . a meal that would have been better without one of the present company. Along with two of his own officers, Beckett had invited Anderson and his surgeon, Towers, to eat with him. Beckett quite liked Towers. At least the man knew when to keep his mouth shut. But Anderson was unstoppable.

161

'I still say we should search the island!'

Beckett blew out the match and eyed the other man wearily. 'And I'd be grateful, Lieutenant,' he said, 'if you'd drop the subject.'

'He's right, Lieutenant,' Towers muttered.

Anderson slammed his fist down, getting to his feet. 'By heaven, Towers . . .' he began.

'Sit down, Lieutenant!' Beckett had stood up himself. 'If this is how gentlemen behave, I'd as soon entertain savages!'

Anderson said nothing but he sat down again and refilled his glass. Beckett sat too and puffed away at his pipe. There was a long, uncomfortable silence in the small cabin.

'You were telling us about your experiences with the Maoris, Mr Beckett,' Towers said.

Beckett relaxed and smiled, and some of the tension left the table. 'Yes,' he said. 'That year we took sixty thousand skins to Port Jackson. There was big money to be made from seals then. We even had Maoris in the crew. But they didn't last.'

'Why not?' Towers asked.

'Just didn't. Who's to say? They killed and ate everyone on the *Boyd*. Been insulted, they said! I've learned to get along with 'em. Speak the lingo . . . that's the answer. Once you can talk to . . .'

He got no further. Anderson was on his feet again and this time he was holding a gun, his face crimson, his eyes wild. 'I've listened to you long enough!' he roared. 'I hold a commission from King George and no tupenny ha'penny trader's going to stop me doing my duty.'

'You can hold a commission from God Almighty for all I care!' Beckett retorted. 'This ain't the English Channel, mister! You're a damned long way from home and I've just about had enough of you.'

Anderson raised the pistol until it was pointing at Beckett's head. 'You'll do as I say,' he said. 'I'm taking over this ship!'

Beckett stared at the pistol, then at Anderson. 'You haven't a chance!' he said. He gestured at the two officers who were already on their feet, closing in on the crazed lieutenant. 'Go on, shoot!' he went on. 'What do you think they'll do to you?'

Anderson glanced at the two officers and in that split second Beckett acted. Leaping on Anderson, he pushed the pistol aside. There was an explosion and a plate shattered. Then Beckett swung a fist. It hit Anderson on the side of the jaw, cracking his lip open and breaking a tooth. Anderson slumped against the bulkhead. Towers sighed and reached for the wine. He had lost count of the number of injuries his master had sustained.

Beckett looked down at Anderson. 'I'd hang you for that if I didn't think you were half-crazed from being so long on that lousy island,' he said. 'But I'm giving you fair warning now, Anderson. Try a trick like that again and you'll swing for it.'

Anderson looked back at Beckett with sullen hatred. But there was nothing more he could do. The two officers were still standing over him. Beckett had the gun. Slowly, he raised a hand and wiped blood from his mouth. 'The privations of the last month have affected me,' he muttered. 'I deserved any punishment you think fit. I lost control and I apologize, Captain Beckett. I give you my word that from now on I'll accept your captaincy.'

'That's good enough for me,' Beckett said.

But it's not good enough for me, Towers reflected as the fallen lieutenant was helped back into his chair. Beckett seemed willing to take Anderson at his word. But Towers knew him better . . .

'That's good enough for me . . .'

Jack Vincent heard the words and smiled to himself in the darkness. Whoever this Captain Beckett was, he was going to regret the day he invited Harry Anderson on board. The thought reminded him that he was himself an uninvited visitor. He had work to do.

He had been doubly lucky that night. First the tide had been against the *Artemis*, so the ship had been forced to anchor off the island. If it had been able to set sail he might never have seen Mason and Pat again. Secondly, there had been no moon. As he and Maru had rowed the jolly-boat around the headland, they had been lost in the darkness. Beckett had posted seamen on the deck, but none had seen the two adventurers climb on board, and none saw them as they crept past the captain's cabin and on down to the brig.

'Holy Saint Patrick! It's Vincent!'

When Jack's face appeared at the barred peephole of the brig, Pat had to pinch himself to make sure he wasn't dreaming. A second later, Mason was trampling all over him in his hurry to get to the door — whether to embrace Jack or to kill him it was hard to say. Li was the last out, his face blank and smiling as if he had actually enjoyed his enforced stay on the *Artemis*.

'Why the . . .?' Mason began.

'Stow it!' Jack whispered. 'Come on!'

They got as far as the upper deck before they were discovered.

The sailors were as surprised to see them as they were to see the sailors. A moment before the deck had been empty, and now here they were, face to face. For a few seconds nobody did anything. Then one of the sailors shouted. Jack hit him. But it was too late.

Six more sailors clambered down towards them — eight against five. Jack drew his cutlass. The first two sailors moved to cover him, one of them drawing a cutlass of his own. Jack slashed forward twice, making a giant letter T in the air. The first stroke disarmed one of the men and disfigured the other. At the same time, Mason picked up the fallen sword and began to lay about him. A third sailor keeled over with a gurgling scream. Blood splattered on to the deck.

Five against five. Now things were even.

But in the cabin, Beckett had heard the commotion. Pulling out his musket, he leapt to his feet and strode over to the door. That was when he discovered that it was locked. The key was in Jack's pocket. Even as he had made his way down to the brig he had been thinking ahead. But Beckett was a large man. With Anderson's curses ringing in his ears, he battered the door with his shoulder. The wood creaked . . .

And at the same time, another nine sailors found their way on to the deck, climbing down the rigging, popping up through the hatches, swarming into the battle area from every direction.

Fourteen against five. Not so good.

But then Maru charged and suddenly there were only thirteen of them as one was pitched over the side and into the water below. Thirteen was an unlucky number for the crew of the *Artemis* for that was when Li decided to take a part in the action.

They had never seen anything like it ... at least that's what the ones who survived would say. The Chinaman moved faster than was humanly possibly. He carried no weapons. But he seemed to fly effortlessly into the air. A foot lashed out, then the side of a hand. Two men fell. He spun round, his left elbow jerking back, his right fist punching forward. There was the unmistakable crunch of bones breaking. One sailor ran at him with a belaying pin. Li seemed only to shimmer. But then the man with the belaying pin was dead and the club itself was in Li's hand.

'Over the side!' Jack shouted.

The seamen of the *Artemis* were hanging back, afraid to take them on. But Jack had heard something that suggested it would be a good idea to get out while they still could. The door of the captain's cabin had crashed open. Beckett had broken through it on the third attempt. And in all the pandemonium, Jack could hear a voice he knew too well. Anderson was shrieking his name, his fury making him almost inarticulate.

He ran forward and cleared the edge of the ship in a perfect dive that carried him over the railings and well out into the blackness of the water. A moment before he went he heard Pat utter a great cry as he jumped himself, holding his nose. Maru, Mason and Li were right behind. They were all away. Then his shoulders and outstretched hands broke through the cool surface of the water and everything was silent as he allowed his own

166

momentum to carry him down. He kicked out and swam forward, enjoying the tug of the water and the utter serenity of this world beneath the surface. Something flew past his head like a wasp and he realized that somebody had shot at him. It would have to be Anderson. Nobody else would have missed.

He took another four strokes before heading back up to the surface and fresh air. When he finally looked about him, the *Artemis* was safely in the distance and Pat, Maru, Li and Mason were swimming towards him. He had anchored the jolly-boat a little further away and soon they were all on board.

'Make for the headland,' Jack ordered as another shot rang out from the *Artemis*. 'The *Sea Wolf*'s anchored there.'

'Will they follow us?' Pat asked.

Jack looked back at the *Artemis*. A few lights burned on board, a flickering yellow against the water. 'Not at night.'

Li nodded. 'Mr Anderson and the captain do not see eye to eye,' he said.

Jack smiled. They had escaped and they were together again. He wasn't to know then that it was for almost the last time.

12

Ragged streaks of pink and silver stretched themselves across the sky. The sun had yet to rise but the clouds were glowing as if with a light of their own, the colours reflecting in the still water below. A solitary seagull floated in the air, silhouetted black against the firmament like a scrap of paper over a bonfire.

Maru saw the seagull, and he understood.

'Take me to my people.'

'What?' Jack was standing at the wheel, only half-awake after a sleepless, watchful night.

'You must take me, Jack.'

'Why?'

'You are my friend. I feel . . .' he touched his heart, '. . . death.'

The seagull uttered a desolate cry and arced away, its wing curving towards the horizon.

The Maoris preferred to die out of doors. To die inside would make that building 'tapu' or forbidden. As soon as the Maori had died and his spirit had been taken to the underworld, led there by the ghosts of his ancestors, the mourning or 'tangi' would begin. Close relatives of the dead man would cut their hair. Some would lacerate their faces with sharp pieces of stone. At last the body would be taken away and buried, surrounded by presents and sitting up like the bodies Anderson had found in the cave.

Maru and the others arrived in the village just as the tangi was finishing. He had been right. The seagull had whispered to him of death: his father's.

A tall, thick-set warrior chief wearing a feather-trimmed cloak stood making a speech as Maru approached. The whole village sat around him. Seeing Maru, they lowered their eyes and looked away uncomfortably. Jack knew at once that something was wrong. The warrior's words confirmed it.

'Kia ora, hoa o nana jurii,' he sneered at Maru. 'Welcome back, friend to the dogs — slave's companion!'

'What's going on?' Pat whispered. 'That feller seems very unfriendly if you ask me.'

'I hang my head in shame that Maru is of the warrior class,' the tall man went on. 'You have disgraced us.'

'My father called me here,' Maru replied.

There was a murmur of sympathy from the villagers.

'Do not hang your head, Tohu,' Maru continued, addressing the warrior. 'I haven't kept company with dogs. These men are warriors too. They are my warriors . . . as are all of you. For I am the son of Tahuru.'

Jack had managed to understand most of what Maru and Tohu were saying. Now he gave Pat a whispered reply. 'Trouble,' he said. 'The other fellow's trying to take over the tribe. Maru's challenging him for the leadership.'

'The village has already chosen its new chief,' Tohu declared. 'It is me — Tohu!'

169

'Since when has a real leader been elected, Tohu?' Maru retorted. 'Kei te kowhai tonu to tuutae!'

The villagers shook their heads as Maru finished with a particularly filthy Maori insult. Maru threw down the spear he was carrying. Tohu picked it up. Mason turned quizzically to Jack.

'It's a challenge,' Jack whispered. 'They're going to fight it out.'

'And what happens to us if Maru loses?'

Jack glanced at the Maoris. He knew that they were responsible for the fight with De Witt and for Maru's subsequent disappearance. Somehow he suspected they wouldn't win any popularity prizes in the village.

'If Maru loses, we run like hell,' he said.

Slowly, Maru closed in on his opponent. Tohu was six inches taller than him, but it was his longer reach that gave him the edge. In the first encounter, his 'taiaha' slammed into Maru's chest, the spearhead flat against the flesh. Maru was thrown to the ground. Then the spear was whistling down, this time point first, aiming for his skull. At the last second, Maru rolled aside. The spear cut a deep hole in the sand, inches away. Then he was back on his feet, holding his weapon in the position that the Maoris called 'popotahi' — vertical to his body.

Tohu attacked for a second time. But this time Maru was ready for him. The point of his taiaha had been half-buried in the sand. As the other warrior charged forwards, he flicked it up. Sand flew into Tohu's eyes, momentarily blinding him. Then, using all his strength, Maru brought the shaft of the weapon crashing round. It hit his opponent in the stomach. Tohu sank to his knees. He tried to get up but he was winded, the strength draining out of him. Maru edged forward, the point of his taiaha hovering above his opponent's throat. The fight was over.

'By rights I should kill you,' Maru shouted in Maori so that all the villagers could hear. 'But you are a fine soldier, Tohu. If you follow me, you will live.'

Tohu looked up at him. 'My shame is too great,' he replied. 'Kill me so that I will die a warrior. If you let me live, I am nobody.'

Maru's fists tightened on his spear and for a moment Jack thought he was going to finish it. But then he stepped back, shaking his head. Tohu got to his feet and released the cloak he was wearing. It slid to the ground. Nobody in the village spoke. Slowly, his head bowed, Tohu walked out.

'Will he take his own life, Jack?' Li asked.

'No. But he'll live a life of shame as a nobody,' Jack said.

Li sighed. 'I think the Chinese way is kinder.'

The other villagers were clustered round Maru now, talking to him in low, earnest voices. Once or twice they glanced back at the pakeha and Jack got the feeling they were talking about them. So this is where we part, he thought to himself. Maru will lead his people. Maybe he'll throw a feast for old time's sake, and then we'll be on our way.

He couldn't have been more wrong.

Maru walked back to them. 'My father died fighting the Ngati Miru,' he announced. 'So now we must take "utu".'

'We?' Jack questioned.

'We — the Ngati Tahururu. And you! Together
. . .'

Jack held up a hand, smiling. 'This is your
fight, Maru. Not ours.'

'I'm not fighting for no savages,' Mason
agreed.

'I have said you will fight.'

Jack saw that Maru was deadly serious and the
smile faded from his face. 'I said I'd bring you to
your people,' he insisted. 'Nothing more.'

'I have said you will fight.'

'Then you'd better say we won't.'

'Maru never goes back on his word.'

While Maru and Jack had confronted each
other, the villagers had closed in around their
new leader, clutching their clubs and spears in
their hands. Jack suddenly felt a dryness in his
throat. There could be no argument. One word
from Maru and . . .

'Out of the frying pan into the fire,' Li muttered. 'I believe that is the expression, is it not
Mr Vincent?'

Lieutenant Harry Anderson was about as
unhappy as Jack Vincent just then.

After the escape from the *Artemis*, he had
pleaded with Captain Beckett to continue the
search across the islands, but Beckett had
refused. He had business of his own, and
Anderson had no choice but to tag along with him
in the bitter knowledge that by the time he
renewed the chase, Vincent could be miles away.

Captain Beckett was dealing in guns, trading
the weapons for land. Towers had been shocked
by the discovery. 'Trading in death,' was how he
put it. But Anderson didn't care. Let these

172

savages wipe each other out! What was it to him? All he could think about was Vincent. Catching Vincent. Killing Vincent. Slowly ... It never occurred to him that his own thoughts were as savage as anything that had ever gone through a Maori's mind.

And there was something he didn't know — something that might have made him a great deal happier if he had. Beckett was trading with the Ngati Miru, the same tribe that had killed Maru's father. Although he didn't realize it, the muskets that were being unloaded from the *Artemis* would be used against Jack and the others. He hadn't escaped. He was still, unwittingly, in the grip of the feud.

'Get those boxes ashore!' Beckett called out.

Anderson was sitting beside Beckett in the long-boat, watching as the beach drew closer. There were about a dozen warriors waiting for them, more Maoris in grass skirts, their faces blank and hostile beneath the swirling patterns. They reached the shore and Beckett sprang out.

'Kia ora, Mahue,' he said.

Mahue was the tallest of the Ngati Miru. He was the only one wearing a cloak. 'Haere mai, e hoa,' he muttered. 'Welcome!'

'I've brought you what you wanted,' Beckett continued in the same language, gesturing at the boxes.

'Good. We'd better go to the Rangatira. He's up there ...'

Mahue pointed and Beckett turned to Anderson with a grin. 'They're pleased,' he said. 'I told you. Give 'em guns and they'll eat out of your hand.'

There were three boxes of muskets. The

seamen carried them through the bush, sweating and straining under the weight, while Beckett chatted cheerfully with Mahue. It was a long journey but never once did Beckett relax his grip on the musket he was carrying. The smile might have rested gently on his lips but all his senses were alert. He had boasted of his friendship with the Ngati Miru, but he still didn't trust them.

At last, when it seemed they had walked four or five miles, he took hold of Anderson's arm. 'There's the river.' He pointed. 'The "pa" is on the other side. See!'

Anderson looked, and despite himself he was impressed.

The pa was a fortified village, built on the side of a hill above the river. Even at a glance, Anderson could see that it was practically impregnable. Two wooden stockades around seven feet high stood outside the village. Behind each one there was a ditch, several feet deep and then a rampart, a mound of earth that rose to the same level as the stockade. A single warrior, standing on the rampart, could easily hold off a whole army as it attempted to climb the stockade. And the whole complex was protected by the river which twisted round it like a natural moat.

'I'm beginning to understand what you mean, Captain,' he said. 'The men who built that would have been a match for Napoleon.'

Beckett grinned. 'They'd have had his grenadiers for breakfast!'

A canoe was waiting for them at the river's edge. Following Beckett, Anderson scrambled towards it. Behind him, the sailors hoisted up the boxes of muskets and began to carry them down.

* * *

'Muskets?'

'Yes. For my warriors.'

There was a feast in Maru's village, but Jack didn't feel like eating. He was sitting next to the new chief beneath a dull, threatening sky with Mason, Pat and the others slightly to one side.

'There are many muskets on the ship,' Maru said.

'I know. I've seen you looking at them.'

'Then you will give them to me?' Jack said nothing, so Maru went on. 'If you do not give them, we will take them.'

'Would you kill to get them?' Jack asked.

'Would you die to keep them?' Maru countered.

'You treacherous heathen!' Mason threw down his bowl and would have thrown himself at Maru had not Li been there to restrain him.

'Shut up, Mason!' Jack said. He turned back to Maru, wanting to argue with him. But the words died on his lips. The young Maori was implacable. He could see it in his eyes. 'Leave us two kegs of powder and four bags of shot,' he said.

Maru grinned and called out to three of the warriors — three of *his* warriors, Jack reminded himself. 'Go to the big white bird,' he said. 'Bring the guns but leave the pakeha two kegs of the sand powder and four kits of the round stones.'

Jack nodded at Pat. 'Go with them,' he ordered.

'Me?' Pat swallowed. 'Holy Mother.'

Mason tried to struggle free, but Li was still holding him. 'We're doomed,' he rasped. 'You've finished us.'

Jack ignored him 'Anything else you want, Maru?' he asked.

175

Maru smiled again but now there was something hard in his face, something that made him look old. 'Utu,' he said.

And at last Jack understood. 'Utu' meant satisfaction or revenge — an eye for an eye, a tooth for a tooth; nothing was more important to the Maoris. Mason might think that Maru had betrayed them, but the thought would never have occurred to the new chief. He had to have utu. That was all that mattered. That was all that ever mattered.

'I ain't risking my life for a bunch of savages!' Mason scowled.

'You've no choice,' Jack reminded him.

'Maru risked his life for us,' Li said. 'To creep away would not be honourable.'

'Or possible,' Jack added wryly.

'So we all go?'

'Not Li.' Jack raised a hand to forestall any argument. 'I want you to guard the *Sea Wolf*, Li,' he said, 'because we're going to come out of this alive.'

The chief of the Ngati Miru was an old man called Haukino. He never seemed to go anywhere in the pa without an entourage made up of village elders and relatives, who spent half the time squabbling among themselves and the rest of it gazing sullenly at their leader after he had told them to be quiet. But they were all smiling now. They had their muskets and Beckett had demonstrated how to use them.

Beckett too was in a good mood. 'I've got my land and he's got his guns!' He slapped a hand on Anderson's shoulder. 'The old monster's so pleased with 'em he's giving a feast in our honour.'

176

'What about Vincent?' Anderson demanded coldly.

'We'll find Vincent later.'

'But you promised me . . .'

'I know these people,' Beckett interrupted. 'You can't rush 'em or they'll shut up tight as clams and then you never get anywhere.' He looked tiredly at Anderson. 'Don't worry,' he reassured him. 'I'll get round to it.'

And that evening, just before the feast, Beckett was true to his word. There was a sense of calm in the pa of the Ngati Miru. They had their guns. They knew how to fire them. They were invincible.

Beckett talked to the old chief for about ten minutes. Then he turned to Anderson. 'He knows about Vincent,' he said.

'Does he know where we can find him?' Anderson asked.

Beckett translated the question and Haukino spoke again. As Beckett listened to the answer, a smile spread across his face. 'That Maori with Vincent,' he said at last. 'He's a chief.'

'What chief?'

'Of the Ngati Tahururu.' Now Beckett laughed outright. 'Don't you see?' he asked. 'You're in luck. They're the ones Haukino wants to fight. His warriors killed their chief . . . and now he says he's going to kill them all. Including Vincent and the rest of them.'

'No!' Anderson's eyes were ablaze. 'Vincent must be brought to justice!' he cried.

Beckett looked at him and slowly shook his head. 'Justice?' he repeated. 'No. You don't want justice. You want revenge! You want him to pay for humiliating you. Well they've got a word for

177

that out here. Do you know what it is?'

'No.'

'Utu. That's why you're after Vincent. You want Utu.'

That same night, Maru led his attack on the Ngati Miru. They crossed the island under cover of darkness — forty warriors plus Jack, Mason and Pat. It was dawn before they reached the other side. As the sun crept over the horizon, they found themselves in a great thermal valley. Pools of mud bubbled at their feet, the steam hovering around them in the strange half-light of the early morning. The smell of sulphur was thick in the air.

'Are you as scared as I am, George?' Pat whispered.

'Shut up!' Mason growled.

'Yes.' Pat nodded. 'I thought you were.'

At last they reached the river. The sun was still low in the sky but it was light enough to be seen. The warriors crouched in the bushes. To look at them you would have thought they had just walked four miles rather than forty. Only the pakehas were sweating and out-of-breath.

Jack gazed at the enemy pa with experienced eyes. Half his life had been spent either in or surrounded by the navy and he knew an impossible challenge when he saw one.

'There's no way you can cross that river without them seeing you,' he told Maru now. 'Not only that — you have no canoes.'

'We shall swim,' Maru said.

'Swim?'

'Like the fish.'

'Underwater?' Mason was too tired to laugh but he still tried.

178

Maru reached forward and plucked a hollow reed. 'No one will see us,' he explained. 'Then we will kill the lookout warriors with the muskets and go into the pa. Then we will kill everyone.'

'Swim underwater? With muskets?' Jack stared at Maru.

'It is easy.'

'No, Maru. It can't be done.'

'It can!'

'You stupid swab,' Mason growled. 'What about your powder?'

Maru looked from Mason to Jack. He didn't understand.

'If the powder's wet,' Jack said, 'the gun won't fire.'

Jack was smiling now. Mason and Pat laughed. But Maru's face was like thunder. He had lost face in front of his warriors. The pakehas were making fun of him! 'You lie,' he exclaimed.

Jack picked up a musket and slid down to the water's edge, being careful to keep out of sight. He ducked the musket under the water and then carried it, dripping wet, back to Maru. 'All right,' he said. 'Kill me!'

Maru took the musket. Slowly he lifted it until it was pointing at Jack. His finger found the trigger. He pulled it. There was a click. Jack shrugged.

'The pakeha pu is no good!' Maru howled. He threw the gun to the ground. 'It is afraid of water.' He took a short stone club and brandished it in front of Jack's face. 'The "mere" is not afraid of water!' He turned to his warriors, switching to their own tongue. 'We shall kill the Ngati Miru with clubs,' he cried. Then, in English, 'And we will fight alone. Not with the pakeha.'

'Thank heaven for that!' Pat muttered.

Jack shrugged. 'Please yourself,' he said.

Maru signalled to his warriors. Quickly, they cut hollow reeds for themselves and moved down to the water's edge.

After the feasting of the night before, the Ngati Miru were asleep. The seamen of the *Artemis*, exhausted by their long journey, slept too. Only one man in the entire pa lay awake.

You don't want justice. You want revenge! You want him to pay for humiliating you. Utu. That's why you're after Vincent. You want Utu.

Beckett's words echoed in Anderson's thoughts. Utu . . . utu . . . the word was like a primitive drum-beat. Had it contaminated him? Had he become nothing more than a primitive savage, lusting after blood?

Suddenly he sat up on his bunk. He couldn't lie there any longer, not with that infernal drum-beat in his brain. Utu, utu . . . He needed air. He needed to clear his head.

He walked outside, crossing the enclosed square of ground that the natives called the 'marae'. He felt better as he walked. Unconsciously, he found himself marching, back straight, arms by his sides. He braced himself in the cold morning air. What had he been thinking about? He was a military man. He always had been. He didn't want revenge. He wanted justice.

That was when he saw the sleeping sentries.

Angrily, he strode over to them. 'You!' he cried. The sentries opened their eyes and regarded him curiously. 'If you were my men, I'd have you flogged!' Anderson bellowed.

The Maori warriors blinked at Anderson, amazed. What was this pakeha doing shouting at them? One of them turned away ... and saw Maru and his men, crouching below the stockade.

The sentry leapt to his feet. 'Ka kokiritia taatou!' he shouted. 'We're being attacked!'

Jack was sitting on the other side of the river with Mason and Pat when he heard the first shots. Whipping out his telescope, he crouched and focused it on the Ngati Miru pa. What he saw horrified him. And yet he had been expecting it.

Maru and his warriors had been caught in the worst possible place. They were in the ditch with their enemies in the stockade above them and a rampart behind them. Their clubs were useless against the muskets of the Ngati Miru. They couldn't go back and they couldn't go forward. They were trapped, and they were being slaughtered.

Jack watched, helpless, as the Ngati Tahururu were torn apart. It had rained some time in the night and their blood was mixing with the water, flowing in miniature torrents through the mud. Jack swung the telescope round and flinched as he saw Maru, shouting and pointing. Then the young Maori seemed to be pulled back by an invisible wire. His hands clutched his stomach. He fell into the mud.

'Maru's hit!' Jack shouted. He handed the telescope to Mason. 'I'm going to get him.'

'You're crazy!' Mason couldn't believe what he was hearing. None of them had ever wanted any part of this war. Maru had tricked them, forced them into coming. And now, just when he could slip away and forget all about it, Vincent was ... 'You're crazy,' he muttered again.

Jack smiled tiredly. 'That's always been my

trouble, hasn't it?' he said. Then he was serious again. 'Go back to the ship.'

Mason sighed through clenched teeth. 'And leave you to die?' he asked.

'We can't . . .' Pat began.

'Listen.' Jack paused as there was another fusillade of shots from the other side of the river. 'That ship is our life-line. Whatever happens, we need her to get out of here. So I want you two on board with Li. Guard her with your lives.'

Mason looked at Pat. Pat looked at Jack. There could be no arguing with him in this mood. They both knew that. 'Aye, aye, sir,' they muttered.

Jack stripped off his shirt and ran down to the river. A moment later he was gone.

Captain Beckett reloaded another musket and threw it up to the Maori warriors who were standing on a wooden fighting platform, firing down into the trench. The chief, Haukino, stood nearby, shouting orders. A wounded soldier was screaming on the other side of the stockade. There was another explosion and the screaming stopped.

'Looks like my merchandise is proving its worth, eh?' Beckett laughed. Anderson snatched up a musket and began to move towards the platform but Beckett grabbed him. 'Keep out of it, Anderson,' he said.

'Let go of me,' Anderson warned.

'I don't want us to be seen,' Beckett snarled. 'Don't you understand, man? When this is all over, I reckon the Ngati Tahururu will be my next customers for guns. And they have land too!'

Anderson wrenched himself free. Beckett

opened his mouth to speak, but then Anderson rammed his musket into the other man's stomach. Beckett toppled over, gasping for breath. Anderson ran towards the ladder.

Jack pulled himself out of the river and ran up towards the pa. He was naked to the waist now, his torso covered in mud, his hair wild. But for the colour of his skin he could almost have been mistaken for one of the natives.

Swerving to avoid the bullets that still thundered down from above, he continued as far as the first, outer stockade. And that was where he found Maru. Someone must have dragged the young chief clear for he was lying there, semiconscious, one hand cupped over his stomach, his face contorted by pain.

'Vincent!'

Anderson had climbed on to the platform. He was only twenty yards away from Jack. The Ngati Miru were still firing all around him. Blood splattered the walls of the pa and lay in puddles all around it.

'Vincent!'

He fired, then threw the musket down in disgust. He had missed. The bullet had coughed in a puddle only inches from Jack's foot.

'Vincent! Vincent!'

Jack scooped Maru up in his arms and carried him back down to the river.

In the pa, Haukino called out an order. It was time to finish it. The gates of the stockade were opened. His warriors ran out, waving their muskets and howling, triumphant.

Jack reached the first of the Ngati Miru's canoes and lowered Maru into it. He couldn't tell

183

now if the young chief were alive or dead. Beneath the dark skin his face was pale and bloodless. His eyes were closed. Jack pushed the canoe out into the river and jumped in himself.

'Vincent!'

Anderson saw Jack escape and screamed out his name yet again. But the gates were open now. The last of the Ngati Miru were being cut apart. And there were other canoes.

Anderson ran forward. Beckett saw him. Some of his sailors began to chase him, 'Let him go!' Beckett shouted. 'It's nothing to do with us.'

Jack's canoe reached the other side of the river.

Anderson, in a second canoe, pulled away from the bank. The oar hit the water, again and again. Utu . . . utu . . . utu . . .

It was time to bring the feud to an end.

Slowly, painfully, Jack struggled up the hillside with Maru in his arms. When he reached the top, Maru opened his eyes. It took him a moment to work out where he was. Then he remembered.

'Leave me,' he whispered.

'Shut up!' Jack ordered and just for once Maru obeyed.

He had seen Anderson behind him. He had no weapon. Anderson would be carrying a sword — probably a musket too.

'Can you walk?' he asked.

Maru nodded. Jack lowered him onto his feet. The two of them ran.

They crossed the thermal valley again, the mud pools heaving and bubbling as if trying to escape from the craters in which they had been born. They followed the frozen rivers of the island, the lava crust that had been petrified a million years before and which would lie there, cold and impenetrable for a million years to come. Their footsteps oozed into the mud and then vanished under a burst of steam. The black rock of the mountains surrounded them. Black smoke from the sulphur pits smothered them, so thick that it was impossible to tell where the smoke ended and the mountains began. And still they ran, Maru groaning, his hand still pressed against his stomach, his fingers caked with dried blood.

At last they could run no more. Maru sank to the ground and Jack knelt beside him, laying his head against the earth. He looked back.

There was a curtain of steam behind him. It was as solid as a sheet of glass only it was opaque, a barrier through which even the sun was unable to shine. But now Jack saw something in the middle of it. A black shape, like a maggot or a worm in a cocoon. It shimmered, took shape . . .

Harry Anderson walked out of the steam.

The chase across the island had changed him. The mud, the steam, the heat and the sulphur had combined to wipe away at last the authority on which he prided himself. His clothes were torn and filthy. Blood streaked his face where a briar had torn him. His shirt hung open. His hair was wild and streaked with dirt, the marks of his previous encounters with Jack were still on him. His collar bone had set badly, bulging to one side of his neck. His face was still pock-marked from the musket that had exploded. In appearance he was no longer the smooth naval officer. In truth, he was barely a man.

'Convict Forty-one!' he screamed.

Jack got slowly to his feet as Anderson approached. The two men stopped only a few feet apart. Anderson was holding his sword. The point was almost touching Jack's neck.

'You never give up, do you, Harry?' he said, wearily.

'I swore I'd bring you to justice.' Anderson's eyes glared madly.

'Still doing it by the book?' Jack tried to smile but he was too tired. It had gone on too long. 'You'll make captain one day.'

Anderson ignored the gibe. 'I'm taking you to Norfolk Island to stand trial for mutiny!' He jabbed forward with the sword. A bead of blood appeared on Jack's skin.

'I'm not coming, Harry.' Jack stood firm, looking down the length of steel and into his enemy's eyes.

Anderson trembled with fury. The point of the sword pressed against Jack's skin again and Jack knew that the lieutenant was fighting with himself, fighting with the temptation to run him through there and then. 'Go on!' he said. 'Why don't you? There's no one to see! Go on! You can forget the rules.'

Forget the rules. It was the one thing Anderson could never even consider. He could torture. He could kill. But only if he did it within the rules. That's what the rules were for. They were there to define the difference between a gentleman and a brute.

With a muffled sob, he threw the sword aside. It hit a rock and slid into the mud. At the same time, he hurled himself at Jack, his hands reaching out for his throat. The two men crashed to the ground.

Maru could only watch, too weak to move. He had never seen anything like this before. The two pakehas were grunting and gasping like animals. Both had taken a terrible beating. It was as if, after failing to destroy the force that bound them together, they had decided that they had no other choice than to destroy each other. Their faces were almost hidden by the blood that covered them. But still they were fighting. And, with a shiver, Maru realized that he no longer knew which was which. Anderson and Jack. Jack and Anderson. They were consumed by their hatred for each other. If they didn't stop soon, it would kill them.

Suddenly Maru realized that they were no longer alone. He twisted round and saw that twenty or thirty men had stepped out of the swirling curtain of steam and were watching the two fighters. Despite his pain, Maru smiled. They were his own people. The Ngati Tahururu. Somehow they had found him. They had come to help him. He would recover his strength and one day he would lead them against their enemies, not to fight for the sake of fighting but to end the war once and for all . . .

Jack saw the Maoris and stopped, swaying on his feet. Anderson waited for him to attack again but he lowered his fists, shaking his head. The Ngati Tahururu were looking at him impassively, as if they were hardly seeing him at all. Nobody moved.

Savages and civilized man. But which was which?

Suddenly Vincent was tired — tired of Anderson and the whole damned business. Every bone in his body ached — and not just from the

187

bruises that he'd sustained. How had he let this happen to him? Here he was on the edge of a new, uncharted world. The South Seas. There was treasure to be found, land to be claimed, friends to be made and treasure to be won. He thought of Sovay with her gypsy eyes, and De Witt and his gold. He remembered Ben Frobisher who had lost himself utterly in the mystery of the islands, and the bosun, John Herrick, who had been true to himself to the end. What was he doing here, fighting this man? He looked at Anderson. The lieutenant was barely able to stand up. His face and chest were glistening with blood. His eyes were swollen. His lip was cracked. Lieutenant Harry Anderson. He was nothing. He never had been.

Jack walked away.

He walked away from the silent Maoris. He walked away from Maru who would be better off with his own people. And he walked away from Anderson. The feud was over. He was ending it.

He walked until he reached the coast and the waves echoed in his ears. Here, at last, the sun shone through. And there was the *Sea Wolf*, its sails unfurled, pure white on a bright blue sea. There were three figures on board, tiny at this distance but looking out for him, waiting. Pat, Mason and Li. His friends.

He was running before he even knew it and then he had plunged into the sea. The cool water washed over him, wiping away the blood and taking all the pain with it. He swam out towards the *Sea Wolf* with the waves roaring in his ears and the sun brilliant in his eyes.

He felt he had left a great weight behind him. He was still alive. And he looked forward now to the adventures that lay ahead. For he was an adventurer. That was what he had always been. And for him, life was the greatest adventure of them all.

BACK TO THE FUTURE BY GEORGE GIPE

He was never in time for his classes . . .

He wasn't in time for his dinner . . .

Then one day . . . he wasn't in his time at all.

Both an exciting novel and a high-spirited adventure film, BACK TO THE FUTURE is the unforgettable story of a modern time-travelling teenager whose journey to the past risks his very own future when he discovers surprises he never could have imagined.

Starring Michael J. Fox, Christopher Lloyd, Lea Thompson & Crispin Glover

Written by Robert Zemeckis & Bob Gale

Music by Alan Silverstri

Produced by Bob Gale & Neil Canton

Executive Producers Steven Spielberg, Kathleen Kennedy & Frank Marshall

Directed by Robert Zemeckis

Amblin Entertainment · A UNIVERSAL Picture

0 552 12774 4   £1.95